Hoop Crazy

The Chip Hilton Sports Series

For more information on
Chip Hilton-related activities and to correspond
with other Chip fans, check the Internet at
chiphilton.com

Chip Hilton Sports Series

#6

Hoop Crazy

Coach Clair Bee
Updated by Randall and Cynthia Bee Farley
Foreword by Bob Knight

BROADMAN
& HOLMAN
PUBLISHERS

Nashville, Tennessee

© 1999 by Randall K. and Cynthia Bee Farley
Printed in the United States of America

0-8054-1988-8

Published by Broadman & Holman Publishers,
Nashville, Tennessee
Page Design: Anderson Thomas Design, Nashville, Tennessee
Typesetting: PerfecType, Nashville, Tennessee

Subject Heading: BASKETBALL—FICTION / YOUTH
Library of Congress Card Catalog Number: 98-28093

Library of Congress Cataloging-in-Publication Data
Bee, Clair.
      Hoop crazy! / by Clair Bee ; edited by Cynthia Bee Farley,
Randall K. Farley.
            p.   cm. — (Chip Hilton sports series ; v. 6)
      Updated ed. of a work published in 1950.
      Summary: A smooth-talking man who claims to have
played basketball with Chip's father creates dissension on
the Valley Falls high school team and plans to use Big Chip's
pottery formula in his latest scam.
      ISBN 0-8054-1988-8 (pbk.)
      [1. Basketball—Fiction. 2. Swindlers and swindling—
      Fiction.] I. Farley, Cynthia Bee, 1952– . II. Farley,
Randall K., 1952– . III. Title. IV. Series: Bee, Clair. Chip
Hilton sports series ; v. 6.

PZ7.B38196Ho   1999
[Fic]—dc21   98-43540
                                                                    CIP
                                                                    AC

1 2 3 4 5 03 02 01 00 99

WILLIAM "DOLLY" KING

Student, athlete, gentleman, and friend

COACH CLAIR F. BEE, 1950

HAL "UPPIE" UPLINGER

Clair Bee's friend and ours

Your devotion, loyalty, and love
came at a critical time
in Clair Bee's life.

That same fellowship continues
through three generations.

With our love,
RANDY, CINDY, AND MIKE FARLEY, 1999

Contents

CONTENTS

Foreword

THERE IS nothing that could be a greater honor for me than to be able to write the foreword to the new editions of the Chip Hilton books written by Clair Bee and revised by his daughter Cindy and son-in-law Randy.

I can remember that, in the early and midfifties, when I was in junior high and high school, there was nothing more exciting, outside of actually playing a game, than reading one of the books from Coach Bee's Chip Hilton series. He wrote twenty-three books in all, and I bought and read each one of them during my student days. His books were about the three sports that I played—football, basketball, and baseball—and had the kind of characters in them that every young boy wanted to imagine that he was or could become.

Chip Hilton himself was a combination of everything that was good, right, and fair in athletic competition. His accomplishments on the field, on the floor, or on the diamond were the things that made every boy's dreams.

Henry Rockwell was the kind of coach that every boy wanted to play for, and he knew how to get the best out of every boy who played for him.

My mother and grandmother used to take me shopping with them in Akron and would leave me at the bookstore in O'Neil's department store with $1.25 to purchase the Chip Hilton book of my choice. It would invariably take me at least two hours to decide which of these wonderfully vivid episodes in athletic competition, struggle, and accomplishment I would purchase.

As I read my way through the entire series, I learned there was a much greater value to what Clair Bee had written than just the lifelike portrayal of athletic competition. His books had a tremendous sense of right and wrong, what was fair and what wasn't, and what the word *sportsmanship* was all about.

During the first year I was at the United States Military Academy at West Point as an assistant basketball coach, I had the opportunity to meet Clair Bee, the author of those great stories that were such an integral part of my boyhood dreams. After all, no boy could have ever read those wonderful stories without imagining himself as Chip Hilton.

Clair Bee became one of the two most influential people in my career as a college coach. I have never met a man whose intelligence I have admired more. No one person has ever contributed more to the game of basketball in the development of the fundamental skills, tactics, and strategies of the game than Clair Bee during his fifty years as a teacher of the sport. I strongly believe that the same can be said of his authorship of the Chip Hilton series.

It seems that every day I am asked by a parent, "What can be done to interest my son in sports?" Or, "What is the best thing I can do for my son, who really has shown an interest in sports?" For the past thirty-three years, when I have been asked those questions, I have always answered by saying, "Have your son read about Chip Hilton." Then I've explained a little bit about the Chip Hilton series.

The enjoyment that a young athlete can get from reading the Chip Hilton series is just as great today as it was for me more than forty years ago. The lessons that Clair Bee teaches through Chip Hilton and his exploits are the most meaningful and priceless examples of what is right and fair about life that I have ever read. I have the entire series in a glass case in my library at home. I still spend a lot of hours browsing through those twenty-three books.

As a coach, I will always be indebted to Clair Bee for the many hours he spent helping me learn about the game of basketball. As a person, I owe an even greater debt to him for providing me with the most memorable reading of my youth through his series on Chip Hilton.

BOB KNIGHT
Head Coach, Men's Basketball, Indiana University

CHAPTER 1

Hoop Crazy

THE TALL, blond forward in the white uniform with red numbers feinted toward the basket and then broke out toward the backcourt where a teammate with powerful legs and broad shoulders was holding the ball. Leaping high in the air, the agile forward took the pass and landed confidently in front of the free-throw line. The stocky black guard, following the pass, cut by his teammate with a sudden burst of speed. The towhead faked a pass to the flying figure, pivoted suddenly, and dribbled toward the basket. The orange-clad opponents converged on the blond player, and for a second it looked as though he might be trapped. But just as his opponents seemed to have him bottled up, the rangy forward leaped high in the air and hooked a fast, accurate pass directly into the hands of his tallest teammate standing unguarded under the basket, and the home team side of the scoreboard flashed to 16.

It was a beautiful play and the home stands roared! Halfway up the bleachers and smack in the middle of the wild Valley Falls High School cheering section, a tall, important-looking man with a small mustache impassively watched the game. He hadn't joined in the cheering, which identified him as a stranger in town. Everybody else in the gym excitedly followed every play in the hot contest between the Big Reds of Valley Falls and the Salem Sailors. The din was deafening, and the stranger breathed a sigh of relief when the Salem captain called time and the noise momentarily subsided.

However, the sheer finesse of the last play captured even the stranger, who elbowed the excited man next to him. "Who is that kid?"

The man knew exactly who the stranger meant. "Why, he's the best basketball player in the state! That's young Hilton! Chip Hilton!"

"Yeah," a man on the other side added, "and a leading scorer in the state too!"

The stranger gravely thanked them and would have withdrawn into his shell, but it was too late now. He'd started something, and they meant to finish it. He got information from all sides.

"Averaging more than twenty points a game, so far."

"Yeah, had ninety-eight up to tonight! Not bad, heh?"

"Got twenty-nine in the first game! The all-time record is thirty-nine."

"Comes by it naturally! His dad set the school record years ago."

"Yeah, there was a big article in the papers several nights ago about it. Didn't you see it?"

The stranger assured them he hadn't read the paper except for the articles regarding the imminent pottery exhibition. The ceramics expo was the reason he was in Valley Falls. Oh, sure he liked basketball. No, he hadn't known Valley Falls was the state champion. Yes, it sure was something that a small town like Valley Falls could be defending champions of such a big state. Yes, the Hilton kid was talented. Yes, he could see that Ch— What was his name? Chip? That Chip Hilton was a team player as well as a scorer. Yes, he surmised Chip was the captain.

The home team dashed back on the floor, and the explosion that greeted them saved him. Play resumed and the stranger was forgotten by the Big Red enthusiasts who surrounded him. Down on the court, William "Chip" Hilton, the focal point of every basketball fan's interest, continued to dominate the game.

The stranger leaned back against the restless knees of the woman directly behind him and concentrated on Hilton. He appreciated expertise in any form, and the basketball savvy of this player was enjoyable to watch. He'd realized this town was keenly interested in basketball when he'd arrived that morning. Printed flyers and hand-painted game posters were everywhere—in the inn where he was staying, in the shop windows, on business doors, and on telephone poles. After he'd elbowed and fought his way into the packed gym, decorated in red-and-white signs and banners, and had sat through the first five minutes of the hectic struggle, there was no longer any doubt in his mind that every Valley Falls resident must be hoop crazy.

The tall stranger liked basketball. Not too many years ago, he'd been a pretty good basketball player himself. In fact, he was still adept at hitting nothing but net. Shooting a basketball was something like riding a bike or swimming. Once learned, the skill was never lost. The graying mustached man had never given up shooting a basketball. He'd stuck to his hobby because he didn't need company, especially since he never stayed long enough in one place to make friends. For years, traveling around the country, he'd dropped into the local Ys and neighborhood courts to practice his shots. It never took him long to draw an audience. If there was one thing he'd learned well when he was much younger, it was how to shoot a basketball. Especially accurate were his old-style, long, one-hand set shots, which had now evolved into jump shots and three-pointers. Sitting there in the stands, he could almost imagine himself in Hilton's shoes. The kid wasn't bad . . .

When the half ended, Valley Falls was leading, 26-20, and the newcomer was again flooded with information about the Big Reds and Chip Hilton. He learned that Henry "Rock" Rockwell, Valley Falls's veteran coach, was the best in the state, and that both Chip Hilton and his best friend, Speed Morris, the black athlete with the rugged build, were three-sport lettermen. The man on the right fished a crumpled schedule out of his pocket and carefully wrote in the scores of the games Valley Falls had played.

"We've won 'em all so far and we're almost certain to win all the rest of 'em. The games with the little stars in front are the teams we gotta beat to win our section. We won't have any trouble doin' that! We've got a lock on the sectional and then it's on to the state championship. You'll see us up in the finals all right! Here, stick this schedule in your pocket and watch our smoke!"

The stranger pretended to study the schedule because it gave him a little relief from the red-hot basketball chatter. He didn't know much about the teams, but it was easy to see the Big Reds had gotten off to a good start.

The second half was almost a repetition of the first. Chip Hilton and the hard-driving guard, Robert "Speed"

HOOP CRAZY

VALLEY FALLS HIGH SCHOOL
BASKETBALL SCHEDULE

Fri.	Nov.	29	Alumni	Home	61-47
Sat.		30	Clinton	Home	52-38
Fri.	Dec.	6	New Benton	Away	49-39
Sat.		7	West Haven	Away	51-47
* Fri.		13	Salem	Home	
* Sat.		14	Delford	Home	
* Fri.		20	Dane	Away	
* Sat.		28	Stratford	Home	
* Fri.	Jan.	3	Dulane	Home	
* Fri.		10	Southern	Away	
* Fri.		17	Parkton	Home	
* Wed.		22	Weston	Away	
* Wed.		29	Steeltown	Home	
* Fri.		31	Northville	Away	
* Fri.	Feb.	7	Hampton	Home	
* Fri.		14	Southern	Home	
* Fri.		21	Steeltown	Away	
* Fri.		28	Delford	Away	

* *Section Two*

State Tournament: March 5, 7, 8 (State University)

Last Year's Sectional Champs and Runners-up

North (Sec. 1)	South (Sec. 2)	East (Sec. 3)	West (Sec. 4)
Waterbury	Weston	Bloomfield	Rutledge
Coreyville	Valley Falls	Edgemont	Seaburg

STATE CHAMPIONS: VALLEY FALLS
RUNNERS-UP: RUTLEDGE

Morris, seemed to be confusing the Salem defense. The speedster would pass the ball to Hilton, follow the pass by cutting to the right or the left of the rangy ball handler, and attempt to drive his opponent into the block set up by the big forward. If Morris succeeded in picking off his opponent on the block Hilton set up, Chip would return the ball to his hard-cutting teammate who would be free for a short, open jumper. If the man guarding Hilton switched to pick up the speeding guard, Hilton would pivot and shoot or dribble in for an easy lay-up.

The stranger shook his head in admiration of the play of these two athletes. They'd obviously practiced their two-man plays hundreds of times. Oblivious now to the frenzied cheering of the fans surrounding him, the stranger began to think about his own days as a basketball player and then about his present predicament. He'd come to the game tonight because he loved basketball, and watching a high school game was an inexpensive way to spend an evening. Tomorrow he'd have to get out to that pottery convention and figure out an angle to raise some quick cash. He sighed and turned his attention back to the court.

Even with Chip and Speed's smooth teamwork the game was no walkover, and the Salem Sailors fought hard. But the poise and experience of the Big Reds were too much for their opponents, and the game ended with Valley Falls chalking up its fifth straight victory, 54-43. On the way out of the gym, through the trophy foyer, and down the long steps to the street, the tall stranger's enthusiastic seatmate kept up a steady flow of conversation—about the game; Chip Hilton; Speed Morris; Rockwell; Taps Browning, the towering junior center; Soapy Smith; Miguel "Mike" Rodriguez; Red Schwartz, Speed Morris's backcourt running mate; even Benjamin

"Biggie" Cohen, the six-foot-four manager. He also talked about J. P. Ohlsen, the owner of the pottery who had given the gym to the town.

"So you're a pottery man too? Well, you've got plenty of company in this town. That's our prime industry in Valley Falls, and about everyone here has worked there one time or another. J. P. believes in community involvement and spirit. Great guy—J. P. Don't miss the exhibit out there tomorrow. You'll see Chip Hilton too. He's got a display, believe it or not! Not his own stuff, but some ware his father made years ago. Kid's father is dead, you know. Got killed in the pottery, saving some guy's life. Big Chip, everybody called him that, was the chief chemist for Ohlsen. Was good too! Graduate of State, and knew his stuff.

"You know, we didn't have Hilton last year. Hurt his leg in football or some accident, and didn't play. Managed the team, though. That's why we're a sure thing to repeat! We've got everybody back from last year plus Hilton! It's a cinch! Well, here's my car. Hope you're going to be in town for the game tomorrow night. Better get here early if you want a seat. Playing Delford! Tough team! Tough coach too! It'll be a knock-down-drag-out game. Guy by the name of Jenkins is Delford's coach. Hates the Rock! Everybody calls Rockwell the Rock. He's our coach, you know. Well, hope to see you tomorrow night."

The stranger said good night and mentally resolved that the Valley Falls gym was one place he wouldn't be found tomorrow night or any other night if he could help it. As he continued along with the crowd, listening to their loud and excited voices, he shook his head in disbelief. Then someone asked how many points Chip Hilton had made and it seemed that fifty voices answered, "Twenty-three!"

"Yeah, eight buckets and a three pointer!"

"And just four free throws—refs shoulda called the fouls on Salem."

"That gives him a 121 for 5!"

"Wait and see what he gets tomorrow night," someone bantered. "Jenkins'll have two men on him!"

"He'll need five to stop Chip!"

The stranger slid behind the wheel of his rental car and shook his head. "It's a disease with these people," he muttered half aloud. "They're hoop crazy!"

CHAPTER 2

Stranger in Town

THE SUGAR BOWL was jammed with the after-game crowd, and Petey Jackson hustled to fill the never-ending stream of orders for pizzas, burgers, shakes, colas, Big Red specials, and banana splits. Busy as Petey was, however, he had time to keep an eye on his star assistant, the one and only Soapy Smith.

"I'm indispensable," Soapy earnestly informed Speed Morris as he crammed a third scoop of ice cream into the tall glass. "Indispensable, Speed, that's all! Here, try this on your taste buds!"

Petey tapped Soapy on the shoulder. "Aren't you basketball guys s'posed to be watchin' your athletic figures?"

Soapy regarded Petey solemnly. "Right!" he agreed.

"Then quit tempting athletes with triple-scoop samples!"

Soapy turned away from Petey and gazed around the crowded fountain incredulously. "Did you hear that?" he sputtered. "Tempting athletes! Me? I'm an athlete, too, ain't I?"

Petey shot him a withering glance. "Someone's been foolin' you. You aren't even on the team!"

Soapy was offended. "What am I doin' on the bench then if I'm not on the team?"

"Taking up room that belongs to the ball boy!"

The laughter that followed Petey's remark didn't seem to worry Soapy. "OK, then I'm a ball boy! At least I'm carrying equipment for the best team in the state!"

That raised a cheer from the whole crowd. Chip Hilton, back in the storeroom where he spent most of his time unpacking deliveries for the Sugar Bowl, as well as for the adjoining drugstore, stuck his head out to see what was going on.

"There's Chip," Soapy cried. "Ask him if I ain't on the team!"

Biggie Cohen wheeled around on the tiny stool that was completely hidden under his 230 pounds. "Hey, Chip," he called, "come here and take care of Soapy."

Chip was soon caught in the middle of Petey and Soapy's argument. In the meantime, the high school customers waited impatiently, facetiously voicing their opinions of the help at the Sugar Bowl and threatening to take their business elsewhere. But the threats had no effect on the three employees. Petey was a full-time employee, while Chip Hilton and Soapy Smith worked part-time. Chip had worked for John Schroeder, the benevolent owner of the drugstore, for several years. Soapy was comparatively new on the job, having taken Chip's place over the summer while Chip was working in Mansfield. Mr. Schroeder had kept him on after Chip's return.

The three friends faced one another now, playfully arguing to the delight of the interested customers who began to order recklessly, secure in the knowledge they wouldn't be served even if their demands did register.

"Where's our twelve pizzas?"

"How about my four banana splits?"

"Gimme three more burgers and fries!"

"Please, may I have a free Coke, you jerks!"

The uproar might have continued until closing time except John Schroeder and Doc Jones strolled in after a leisurely walk following the game. In a second, three employees were falling all over one another, each trying to fill the same order. But Doc Jones and John Schroeder didn't seem to notice anything unusual and shouldered through the crowd to the storeroom.

At 11:30, Chip, Soapy, and Biggie started home. Taps and Speed were waiting at the curb.

"Another minute and you'd have had to walk home," Speed chided. "Don't you guys ever quit?"

Taps grumbled, shivering, "This isn't July, you guys!"

Speed waved a hand grandiloquently to Taps. "Open the door for these fine gentlemen, Taps."

Browning bent his six-foot-seven-inch frame nearly to the ground in a deep bow and opened the door on Speed's red mustang.

The basketball hopes of Valley Falls rode in that overloaded car. Chip Hilton, the Big Red captain and high scorer, was a tall, lanky kid who weighed in at 180 pounds.

Speed Morris, Hilton's chief running mate, owned the sleek fastback. Morris was a solid five-ten with speed to burn. He hit 170 pounds and created the spark of the hoop squad. A hard dribbler and a good passer, Speed was the backcourt quarterback who initiated most of the offensive plays and was responsible for the defensive balance of the team.

The shortest of the crew, redheaded, freckled-faced Soapy Smith, was five-feet-eight and inclined to be chunky. But he wasn't slow, he wasn't lazy, and he was a good basketball player with a smooth shot. Soapy was ambitious some of the time, happy most of the time, and irrepressible all of the time.

Taps Browning, Chip Hilton's elongated shadow, was extremely slender and Valley Falls's star center. Although he weighed only 170 pounds, his frame was large and was beginning to show signs of filling out. Taps was the youngest in the crowd and the only one who wouldn't graduate in June.

The last, but certainly not the least, was 230 pounds of athletic muscle and warm heart. Benjamin "Biggie" Cohen had been the anchor man of the Big Red football and baseball teams ever since he entered Valley Falls High School. He'd played baseball for three years—in the outfield the first year and then replacing Hilton at first base when Chip had first moved to catcher and then changed to pitcher. Cohen threw left-handed and was a power hitter.

Hilton and Morris had been three-letter men ever since their first year in high school and had tried to get Biggie on that list by encouraging him to play basketball. But the round ball didn't have enough handles for Biggie. Hilton and Morris hadn't given up, though, and had finally achieved their goal by asking Coach Rockwell to appoint Cohen manager of the varsity team.

"Guess we doused the Sailors, all right," Soapy reveled.

Taps Browning yelled happily, "Number five for the record!"

Biggie Cohen cheerfully elbowed Soapy. "And thirteen to go," he roared. "Thirteen!"

A few minutes later, Speed downshifted the three-speed and rolled into the Hilton driveway. The noisy passengers piled out and barged up the walk, onto the porch, through the unlocked door, down the center hall, and into a big, comfortably furnished family room where Chip's mother was reading a book with a purring Hoops curled up at her feet.

The noisy intrusion didn't surprise Mary Carson Hilton. She was used to these sudden visits by Chip's friends. The Hilton home, long the center of activities for a group of athletic-minded high schoolers, was always open to Chip's friends.

Sunday dinners after church and after-game snacks provided Mrs. Hilton with one of her greatest pleasures. She enjoyed having Chip and his friends liven up their home. Tonight, her smiling gray eyes were joyfully proud as she kissed her son and patted him on the shoulder.

"You played great tonight, Chip," she said happily.

"I'll say he did," Biggie said admiringly. "Twenty-two points!"

"Should've had more," Speed growled. "He passes off too much. We have to fight with him to get him to shoot."

"Yeah," Soapy grumbled, "he acts like he ain't s'posed to shoot! His shootin' average is better'n 45 percent! The rest of us can't hit better'n one out of three! Hey, wonder what's on the Hilton menu?"

Without waiting for an answer, Soapy bolted from the room with Taps and Hoops right behind him. The others followed, but before they reached the kitchen, Soapy was bellowing: "What's this? We gonna eat off Indian pottery?"

Richly colored clay bowls, plates, and vases of all sizes covered the kitchen counters.

"What's this all about?" Speed asked.

Mary Hilton laughed. "It's Chip's idea. This is the ware he's going to exhibit tomorrow at the pottery convention."

"You mean sell, Mom," Chip said, "at least try to sell."

While the others talked, Biggie examined several of the pieces, carefully estimating the weight, the finish, and the texture of the clay. He nodded approvingly: "This is nice stuff, Chip. You didn't—"

Chip shook his head vigorously, exchanging glances with his mother.

"Chip's father made it years ago," Mrs. Hilton explained. "It's been up in the attic all this time, and Chip thought perhaps he could sell it and add the money to his college fund."

"Not all of it," Chip corrected. "I'm going to keep some of the best pieces. I've got them down in the lab in the basement."

His college fund was serious, and it wouldn't be long until he'd need money for tuition, dorm, books, and meals. Eight months fly by pretty fast.

"Hey guys," Soapy interrupted, "Hoops is hungry, and I didn't come here to talk about pots!"

The message was clear. Bring on the food.

After the tall newcomer had left the basketball crowd, he drove from one end of Main Street to the other before returning to the Valley Falls Inn. He sat in the lobby listening to the visiting pottery men and women talk and trying to figure a way out of his financial predicament. He had a strong hunch that things were going to break for him in this town! A little later, he made his way to his room, locked the door carefully, and inspected the window overlooking the first-floor porch.

He grabbed the TV remote and switched on the local news before placing his keys, knife, watch, overextended credit cards, and a slim roll of bills on the nightstand and slowly undressing. He snapped off the light and, sitting there on the side of the bed, slipped the watch and the roll of bills into the toe of one of his socks and tucked it under his pillow. He hefted the key ring and felt the odd assortment of keys attached to it. He smiled grimly as he jingled them softly. They were about as important as money . . . in his business.

He reached under the pillow and placed the keys in the sock and slipped the sock back under the pillow before climbing into bed. You couldn't tell about small-town hotels, and that thin roll of bills represented all the money in the world to him right now. He remembered when the roll he carried was a thick one. But things had been tough lately, and the money was slipping away. Well, he'd think of something tomorrow. He'd *have* to think of something pretty soon.

The stranger was a pottery man of sorts and had been around potteries all his life. Mostly, however, he lived by his wits. He'd come to Valley Falls to try to maneuver an opportunity out of the convention and exhibit. His thoughts drifted back to the basketball game and the big, blond kid. That disturbed him—thinking about basketball and basketball players when he should be thinking about a slant to raise money.

He'd been a pretty fair basketball player himself not too long ago. He hadn't been much of a team player then, and he wasn't much of a team player now. He'd rather go his way alone. Funny about basketball, though. He'd always been a sure shot. He clasped the long fingers of his soft hands together. Guess he couldn't do much with those hands except shoot baskets or manipulate locks. He chuckled in the dark. Well, it was a lot easier to let other chumps do the work. Why get calluses when he could use someone else? He'd better get busy, though, or he might have to go to work after all.

Early breakfasts were the norm at the Hilton home, and Chip was up at 6:00 making last-minute preparations for his exhibit. Mary Hilton, a supervisor with the telephone company, left home about 8:00 and Chip wasn't expected at the Sugar Bowl until 7:30, but breakfast was always ready at 7:00.

Chip could make the Sugar Bowl in ten minutes, and by 8:30 on school days he had his work finished. Today he wanted to get away early so he could get his ware down to the pottery recreation center in plenty of time. He fed Hoops, hurried through his breakfast, and then hustled down to the Sugar Bowl. By 7:30 he had everything in order.

The pottery recreation center was bustling with activity when Chip arrived, and he was soon busy arranging his dad's ware on the display table Abe Cohen, Biggie's older brother, had assigned to him. The doors opened at 9:00, and it seemed to Chip that every person in Valley Falls, and in the state, too, was there.

Chip's ware didn't last long. He sold all but two of the pieces in the exhibit before 11:00. The eagerness of the buyers almost tempted him to go home and get a few more pieces, but he put that thought out of mind. He was determined to keep those beautiful examples of his father's handicraft. They were now safely locked away in the lab Big Chip had built in the basement, and they were going to stay there.

The tall stranger arrived early too. He whistled in admiration when he saw the building J. P. Ohlsen had built for his employees and the community. Ohlsen had really splurged when he built this recreation building. In addition to a cafeteria, library, exercise rooms, several bowling lanes, a billiard room, a reading room, and a small theater, the building boasted a fine gym and a large multipurpose room where today's exhibit was being held.

After the newcomer had inspected the building, he wandered from booth to booth examining the ware. He covered the room thoroughly, covertly studying the men and women, appraising them shrewdly and cataloging each in his mind. He contrived to be busily engaged in examining a piece of ware close to whatever group was talking pottery. One group interested him particularly. They were older, obviously prosperous, and their talk stamped them as experts in ceramics. He moved closer and listened intently as they minutely examined a small piece of ware.

"It's beautiful," one of the men said approvingly.

"I haven't seen anything like that for a long, long time. Where'd you get it?"

"From the tall, blond kid over at that corner table. Said his father made it years ago in his home lab."

"You never see that kind of quality anymore. Can't get the clay!"

"Nor the chemists either."

"You've got something there!"

"I guess Ohlsen would pay dearly to obtain some clay and a formula or two that could turn out this kind of ware."

"I believe you're right! He's going to have to do something and do it quick. He isn't getting the kind of clay he wants from England now, and I understand he's planning to try something new next year. His team of chemists is working overtime on domestic clays and new formulas."

"There he is now, talking to the teenager who sold me this work."

The stranger replaced the piece of ware that he'd been examining while he listened to the conversation of the out-of-town potters and sauntered away. As he casually moved from table to table and in the direction of Chip's table, he carefully checked out the tall man who was sponsoring this exhibit and who was so prominent in the field of ceramics. Then, as if struck by a sudden thought, he stopped abruptly and snapped his fingers. His eyes narrowed and his face was lighted by a sly smile. This was the angle! Ohlsen was the ticket . . . wealthy . . . desperately seeking a new formula or a source of clay . . . ripe for a picking . . . Why fool around with small stuff when he could land something big?

J. P. Ohlsen was a friendly man. Tall and lanky, he carried himself with poise and assurance, indicating confidence and strength. His stern face initially gave the impression of a cold nature, but after a short time everyone knew he was a good man who believed in honesty in business as well as in sports. He was in a hurry, but he took time to stop by Chip's display for a friendly word. J. P. Ohlsen liked Chip Hilton. He liked the spirit and the ambition this tall, good-looking kid with the level gray eyes displayed in his work, in his studies, and in his play.

"Looks as though you're pretty well sold out, Chip," he said with a chuckle. "Is that all you have left?"

"No, sir." Chip said quickly. "I've got some more that Dad made at home, but that's not for sale! I'm working with some of Dad's old formulas and trying to make a few pieces myself."

Ohlsen's eyes lighted with pleasure. "You mean your dad's lab in the basement is still there?"

"Yes, sir! Everything still works too. Of course, I'm not very good, and I have a lot of trouble figuring out the formulas Dad created, but I have a lot of fun trying."

Ohlsen was nodding his head as Chip talked, but his thoughts were far away. Absentmindedly he wished Chip good luck and walked away. He was thinking of another Hilton, the Hilton who had been his chief chemist and who had lost his life trying to save a careless workman when this teenager was just a little boy. Life moved fast. Ohlsen thought back over the years when Bill Hilton had come back to Valley Falls with his university degree and a head full of great ideas about pottery and clay and formulas. Bill had moved fast too—right up to chief chemist. Ohlsen's face tightened as he thought of the fine work Hilton had done and the progress the plant had made in those early days. He needed a Bill Hilton now.

The tall stranger had maneuvered so that he overheard the entire conversation between Chip and J. P. Ohlsen. When Ohlsen left, the newcomer headed toward the exit. He was all set now. The plan that had been rapidly taking shape in his agile mind was practically complete, and the first step was clear. His Valley Falls coup depended to a great extent on making the acquaintance of Chip Hilton and getting a peek at that laboratory and those formulas in the basement of the Hilton home.

CHAPTER 3

Twenty-One Passes

THE VALLEY FALLS public library was small, but it carried in its archives just about everything that had ever happened in the town or to one of its citizens. The tall man with the graying mustache lost no time in securing the newspaper files. He concentrated on the *Times* and the *Post*. He spent the entire afternoon and evening making notes about the life and times of Big Chip Hilton.

Oblivious to everything but his task, Baxter didn't notice the time until it was too late for him to make the basketball game. Still, he felt satisfied; he'd completed a fine day's work. Now he'd go to bed and fit the information he'd gleaned into the plan rapidly taking shape in his mind.

Baxter was reviewing some of the things he'd have to memorize. Hilton had been a three-letter man in Valley Falls High School and in college. He'd been a halfback in football, a high-scoring forward in basketball, and a catcher in baseball. A major league prospect.

Oh, yes, he mustn't forget Hilton had been given the trophy basketball by his teammates the very first time Valley Falls had won the state championship. Both papers had printed a photograph of the serious-eyed athlete, so remarkably like his son, holding the championship ball.

Baxter quickly dropped off to sleep, his mind at ease now that he'd mapped out his plan. J. P. Ohlsen was definitely cast in the role of the Valley Falls fall guy in his newest get-rich-quick scheme.

It was just as well the stranger didn't try to make the Valley Falls–Delford game. He wouldn't have had a chance. Ohlsen Gym was packed by 6:00. In fact, there was such a crowd that some of the season ticket holders found it impossible to get to their seats and had to stand throughout the game. This was a grudge game.

The noisy crowd was talking it up even before the junior varsity teams took the floor.

"S'pose Jinx and Rock will tangle tonight?" someone asked excitedly.

"Wouldn't be surprised!"

"Remember two years ago when Jenkins hit our manager?"

"Aw, he didn't hit him; he pushed him!"

"Well, pushed, then. What was that kid's name?"

"Greg Lewis, wasn't it?"

"Yeah, that's right!"

"Rock did all right the last time they tangled!"

"Well, I got me a ringside seat for this one!"

"Think Browning can hold that big Henry kid? I don't!"

"So what! Think Delford can hold Chip Hilton?"

Little by little the loud talking dwindled away. The crowd slowly moved from the lobby into the gym toward the reserved seats and the bleachers, then into the aisles, and finally to the very floor itself where they stood just outside the sidelines and baselines of the court.

For the first time in their young careers, the Valley Falls JVs played to a capacity house. The JV games normally began at 6:30, and usually only their parents and friends were there to cheer the Little Reds on to victory. But not this night. Every inch of spectator space in Ohlsen Gym was covered. The JVs responded nobly, playing as though they were the feature attraction. Scottie Peck and Adam DeWitt were particularly outstanding. Chet Stewart, JV coach and assistant to Henry Rockwell, watched in amazement as his players completely submerged the Delford team by a score of 42-26.

While the JV game was in progress, the Big Reds were preparing for the coming battle. Chip was sitting quietly in front of his locker, conserving all his strength and thinking about the approaching game. Delford's big Red Henry was averaging thirty points a game and that meant trouble. Then there was Jenkins, the Delford coach, known for his unethical character and poor sportsmanship. Why would a board of education keep an individual as cordially hated by every team that played Delford?

Worst of all, Delford's players took after Jenkins. They played rough and dirty. When the officials weren't looking, they would hold opponents' uniforms, trip them, and elbow them in the ribs if they turned their backs. Rock was wise to this, though, and always warned his team that Jenkins used those tactics to get the other teams to lose their cool, start retaliating, and sometimes get thrown out of games. Rock said that defeating a coach or a team like that was the best way to even up the score.

Chip heard a burst of cheers and he knew Delford was on the floor. A moment later, he was on the court dribbling toward the south basket. The frenzied cheering from the Big Reds fans drowned out Delford's rooters, his thoughts, and just about everything else. Squeezed together in the stands, the Brownings, Mrs. Morris, and Mary Hilton, all dressed in Valley Falls red and white, cheered with the crowd:

"YEAAAAA VALLEY - YEAAAAA FALLS
FIGHT! TEAM! FIGHT!"

Chip's teammates followed him toward the south basket. While Dink Davis led the cheering squad and the fans through a series of cheers, Chip and his teammates went through Rockwell's warm-up drills with pep and precision. Their crisp passes and expert shooting evoked roars of appreciation from the fans.

On the other side of the court, "Jinx" Jenkins, his face sullen and flushed as usual, watched every movement of Chip and his teammates. Jenkins stood in front of the visitors' bench with his feet spread wide apart and his hands on his hips. His posture mirrored his belligerent nature.

The referee summoned Chip to the center circle where Red Henry joined him. Chip was six-foot-two, but he had to look up to meet the Delford captain's eyes. They matched hard grips and eyed each other steadily as the referee ran through the usual pregame talk.

"Captain does the talking for the team. Game's the usual four eight-minute quarters. Ball's in play at all times unless it hits the basket supports or the back of the board. Watch the lines when you're inbounding the ball.

We're going to call it if you crowd the man out of bounds. Guess that's it. Let's have a clean game!"

Chip extended his hand again, but Henry ignored it and turned abruptly away to join his teammates and Jenkins at the side of the court. Rockwell was waiting for Chip. After a brief word and a silent grip of six right hands, the team's voices chorused, "Let's go!"

Red Henry got the tap and it was Delford's ball, with the possession arrow set toward the Valley Falls basket. The visitors formed their attack leisurely, and Chip matched his opponent's steps with a long drag slide that kept his feet in position for a quick start. Henry had moved to a position on the free-throw line, and Taps Browning was playing him cautiously, keeping a short distance away so he could switch if Delford attempted a pick or tried to split the post.

But Delford wasn't trying any fast-moving plays. Their strategy was just the opposite. They passed and cut, passed and cut, using a roll attack that carried the four players moving the ball from one corner to the other and then back again. Chip, Speed, Red, and Mike kept walking and sliding with each roll, expecting their opponents to suddenly drive or cut to the basket. But nothing happened, and it dawned on Chip that nothing was going to happen. Delford was going to slow down the game, hold the ball, use a freeze attack. Jenkins had figured a low-scoring game was his best chance to win, and he was attempting to make it a *very* low-scoring game.

Chip thought it over and started to call for a time-out but realized he couldn't call time until Valley Falls had the ball or the ball became dead. From the Delford bench Jenkins's bellow of "move, move, move" became monotonous, and the Big Reds continued to slide while Delford continued to pass and cut, pass and cut, and pass and cut.

When the crowd realized the situation and understood the strategy Jenkins was using, the cheering changed to one continuous roar. That's the way it went until the crowd picked up the count and began to chant every time Delford passed the ball.

"Fourteen, fifteen, sixteen, seventeen, eighteen, nineteen, twenty, twenty-one!"

There was a sudden lull on the count of twenty-one. Catching Taps asleep, Henry immediately spun to the basket, hauled in a pass, and scored the first basket of the game. Chip called time!

The stands were buzzing now, and in the huddle Chip was buzzing too. "Look, guys, they're freezing the ball, using a delayed attack, and that means they won't take a bad shot. Let's play 'em a little loose and sag whenever we're away from the ball and try to clog up the middle. OK? Another thing! On the offense we'll work for good shots too. Close ones, sure ones! OK? Let's go!"

While Delford had been employing its stalling game, the continuous roar from the stands had made it tough on Stan Gomez, WTKO's local announcer. Now the time-out gave him a chance to explain to his listeners what was happening. It gave Petey Jackson a chance to hear something on the radio in the Sugar Bowl besides the bellowing crowd of hoop-crazy fans.

"Yes, it's a tough place to work a game, and I know you didn't get much of that first minute of play. As I said before, this is a tough place to work a game, here at the scorer's table, with the cheers and boos and yelling practically silencing his play-by-play. But it can't be helped, and I'm hoping you'll stay with us.

"The counting you heard was the crowd counting the number of times Delford passed the ball before they took a shot.

"They passed it twenty-one times before they took a shot! Delford now leads 2-0. And fans, that passing and the shot that ended it consumed exactly one minute and five seconds.

"Valley Falls called time-out. It'll be their ball out of bounds at the north end of the court. There's the horn and the ball's about to be in play again. Guess I'll have to start yelling again.

"Morris passes the ball to Schwartz, now to Rodriguez. He's dribbling down the right side of the court. There's a pass to Hilton. He passes it back out. Morris has it, over to Schwartz on the far side of the court, back to Browning at the free-throw line. Now back out to Morris right here in front of us. Morris dribbles and hooks it in to Hilton in the lane, and Hilton scores!" The announcer's voice rose to a shriek.

The roar that had preceded the time-out and had slowly gained in volume suddenly overwhelmed Stan Gomez's voice. Baxter switched off the game and glanced at his wrist watch. He knew that ball games weren't won in the first or the second or the third quarters but in the last quarter. Besides, he needed to do some thinking.

It was all over when Baxter turned the radio back on. The announcer's hoarse voice cracked against a background of steady cheering.

"And so there it is fans, 41-34. But don't be fooled by that score. It was a tense game all the way. There was more basketball packed into this one game than there was in last year's entire tournament at State.

"The first half ended with a dull 10-10 score. Then in the third period Coach Jenkins of Delford changed his slow-moving offense to a pressing attack, which carried Delford to a 33-21 lead at the end of the third quarter.

But Coach Henry Rockwell had one up his sleeve too. He sent the Big Reds back into that final stanza fighting mad. The biggest Red of them all, basketballwise that is, Chip Hilton, went point crazy and scored—get this now—a tremendous twenty points.

"Yes, I know exactly what you're thinking. Impossible! But you're dead wrong. It's in the book—twenty points in eight minutes!

"Too bad Hilton didn't start his scoring a little earlier. He might have broken the Big Red scoring record of thirty-nine points.

"And say, friends, do you know who holds the Big Red scoring record for a single game?

"You don't? Well, you ought to know; the name's the same. Yep, Hilton. Chip's father. Bill Hilton, Big Chip to some of you, scored thirty-nine points in a game against Dane twenty-five years ago.

"So, the final score is Valley Falls 41, Delford 34.

As the two teams headed to the locker rooms, Mary Hilton's eyes followed her son's retreating figure. She stood with a wistful smile, the old ache catching in her heart, thinking back through the years, oblivious to everything except the emotion misting her gray eyes. "Our son," she whispered. "Our wonderful son."

CHAPTER 4

The Hook Is Set

MARY HILTON peered over Chip's shoulder at the story of the Delford game in the *Post*. Chip stirred restlessly. "Aw, Mom, I wish you wouldn't believe everything you read in the papers!"

"Pete Williams says you were the difference between the two teams! You said yourself Pete Williams is the best sportswriter in town."

"Who wouldn't after stories like that!"

"Joe Kennedy says the same thing in the *Times!* They both can't be wrong!"

Mrs. Hilton gently pulled the paper out of Chip's reluctant hands and sat down to enjoy what Pete Williams had to say about the game and about her son.

BIG REDS SHELLAC DELFORD
IN "BATTLE OF WITS"
SEESAW GAME WON IN LAST QUARTER
Hilton Scores 26
Valley Falls's state champions defeated Delford
last night in a record last-quarter scoring spree to win

THE HOOK IS SET

41-34. William "Chip" Hilton was the difference in the two teams as they battled on even terms through the first half to an incredibly low 10-10 score.

Delford's first-half tactic of holding the ball on the offense was unexpected, and Valley Falls fans were in a near-frenzy when the locals seemed unable to match the strategy. Delford has been one of the high-scoring teams of the state this season, and local fans were all keyed up for a basket barrage. They got it, but not until the final quarter!

Delford set the pace of the first half when big Red Henry got the tap and then joined his teammates in passing the ball exactly twenty-one times before a shot was attempted, resulting in the first score of the game.

Coach Jenkins changed his tactics in the third quarter, forcing the play by pressing the Big Reds all over the court. When the fireworks were over, Delford led 33-21. It looked like the state champs were going to receive their first defeat of the season.

The final quarter was the wildest ever seen at Ohlsen Gym. The Big Reds, sparked by Hilton, suddenly caught fire and swarmed all over the visitors—intercepting passes, forcing turnovers, and using Delford's own third-quarter tactics to dominate the play and pull up even in the score. Hilton, shooting with uncanny skill, poured in six straight goals in four minutes to tie the score at 33. Delford called time, and Jenkins gave instructions to resume their first-half strategy of holding the ball.

Rockwell countered this by calling time himself, and when the Big Reds came out of the huddle, it was to continue their forcing style to swarm all over Delford. Before Jenkins could sit down, Chip Hilton stole the ball to score and put Valley Falls in the lead for the first time. Thereafter, it was all Hilton. He scored on a jump shot from the free-throw line, again on a follow-up, pivoted around when his opponent passed the ball in from out of bounds, and intercepted the ball to score again. Hilton's last four points were made in exactly seven seconds, and that brought the Big Red total to 41 and Hilton's personal point total to 26. The final score: Valley Falls 41, Delford 34. Delford scored exactly one point in the final quarter while Hilton scored all of the Big Reds' points, exactly 20, to set a new state mark.

Hilton has now scored a total of 147 points in six games for an average of slightly over 24 points per game. With Hilton in the lineup, the Big Reds have a good chance of retaining the state title. Hilton didn't play last year due to a leg injury. But his exploits on the diamond last spring and on the gridiron this past fall prove he's as strong as ever. And with two good legs and the hands and shooting eye Chip possesses, all existing sectional and state scoring records are likely to be shattered.

The box score:

Valley Falls/FG		3FG	FT	PF	T
Hilton, f	11	0	4	1	26
Morris, g	1	1	1	2	6
Browning, c	0	0	1	4	1
Rodriguez, g	1	0	0	4	2
Schwartz, f	1	0	1	1	3
Smith, g	1	0	0	0	2
Peters, g	0	0	1	1	1
English, c	0	0	0	3	0
Totals	15	1	8	16	41

Delford / FG		3FG	FT	PF	T
Lando, f	3	0	1	3	7
Helms, f	1	0	0	2	2
Henry, c	5	0	7	1	17
Tatum, g	0	1	0	4	3
McBride, g	0	0	2	1	2
Cole, g	1	0	0	0	2
Parry, f	0	0	1	2	1
	10	1	11	13	34

THE HOOK IS SET

While Mary Hilton was reading about the Delford game, Chip was reading the front-page story on the pottery convention. The story gave the history of the local pottery and J. P. Ohlsen's contribution to both the industry and to Valley Falls. Chip finished the article and his thoughts jumped from pottery, to basketball, to figuring how much money he now had in his college fund. Then he got to thinking about the mortgage still remaining on the house. He knew his father had loved this big old house, and he knew his mother loved it just as much. She'd told him many times how his father, just before he'd lost his life at the pottery, had battled the mortgage and the expensive illness of his only brother. Chip knew his mother's job at the Valley Falls phone company had paid a modest income and had barely been sufficient to meet the little family's expenses.

Chip knew, too, that Valley Falls was blessed with a hometown bank controlled by local interests. The members of the board kept extending the loan until, finally, Mary Hilton had been promoted to supervisor. Then the payments on the mortgage had been resumed.

The remaining mortgage on the house was still considerable, but Chip and his mother could see daylight now. As he sat there, Chip was trying to figure out some way he could turn the college fund over to his mother to apply to the mortgage and find some other way to cover his college expenses. Every time he'd brought that up before, his mother had been hurt and had said his college education meant more to her than twenty houses, and so that was that.

Chip was in a reflective mood now, and when he got that way at home, he liked to work in his father's lab. He unlocked the lab door and sat down to think some more about his future hopes and plans. Chip had wanted to follow in his father's footsteps—to study chemistry and someday, maybe, be J. P. Ohlsen's chief chemist at the pottery. But sports meant so much to him that he'd also dreamed of becoming a coach or a sportswriter.

His mother's quick footsteps on the floor above brought his thoughts back to the present, and he began examining the pieces of ware he had decided to keep. Mr. Browning, their next-door neighbor, was in charge of the mixing department at the pottery, and he'd assured Chip that these pieces were superbly molded and of excellent quality. Chip's jaw squared as he looked at them. One thing was sure, college or no college, mortgage or no mortgage, he'd never sell them. He returned them to the shelf and then began to browse through the typewritten formulas filed so carefully in the top drawer of the cabinet.

Baxter was up early that Sunday morning too. He'd arrived at a plan of action that he hoped would gain him access to the formulas and ware in the Hilton home. The kid was the answer to that problem. He'd get to know the kid and use him as a key to the Hilton home. Well, the kid was all wrapped up in basketball, and Baxter was certainly well qualified to talk basketball.

It wasn't strange that the newcomer to Valley Falls ended up at the Sugar Bowl that Sunday afternoon. He was disappointed to find only Petey Jackson and his little brother, Paddy, in the store. In a way that turned out to be an opportunity, for if there was one person in the world who was completely hoop crazy, it was Petey Jackson. A few cautious remarks and Petey and his customer were on like old friends.

"This seems to be quite a basketball town," Baxter commented guardedly.

"Seems to be," Petey echoed, "seems to be!"

"Yes, what do you mean *seems* to be?" Paddy parroted.

"Just judging from the enthusiasm and the big write-ups the games get in the papers. But that's all right with me. I played a lot myself!"

Paddy's attitude changed instantly. "You play now?" he asked, his blue eyes opening a little wider.

"No, I just fool around now, but I'm a pretty good shot!"

Paddy accepted that challenge immediately. "Bet you can't shoot as good as Chip," he said truculently.

The stranger lifted a condescending eyebrow. "Never heard of him."

That was too much for Paddy. "We never heard of you either," he blurted, rubbing a lock of red hair out of his eyes. "What's your name?"

The stranger smiled, amused. "Baxter. T. A. K. Baxter," he announced softly.

Petey shook his head and eyed the stranger appraisingly. "You know something," he said slowly, "Chip Hilton's the best shot I ever saw. He's all-state. If you never heard of him, I don't think you know anything about basketball at all."

Paddy shook his head. "Never heard of Chip?" he muttered. Then he turned to the stranger, again on the attack. "Where'd you play basketball?" he demanded.

"For the university," Baxter responded nonchalantly, "up at State!"

"At State!" Petey sputtered. "You must've been there about the same time Chip's father played. Did you know him? Big Chip Hilton?"

The stranger looked at Petey with surprised eyes and with his lips slightly parted. After a short pause, he shook his head reluctantly. "No," he breathed, shaking his head again, "it can't be. Too much of a coincidence. The Bill Hilton I knew—"

Suddenly he jumped up from his stool. "Come to think of it, though, he was from this part of the state. I wonder—"

Petey wasn't wondering. He knew. "Look, Mr. Baxter," he declared confidently, "there was only one Big Chip Hilton that ever played at State! And that was our Chip Hilton's dad."

The stranger seemed completely nonplused. "I can't believe it," he said slowly. "It just can't be!"

Baxter definitely appeared greatly moved. He walked slowly to one of the tables and dropped heavily to a chair. "Let me see," he reflected, "sixteen, seventeen, that would make it about twenty years ago." He slapped the top of the table. "It could be, it could be. I'd sure like to meet that kid."

"That's easy," Petey advanced eagerly, "you just get down here anytime tomorrow evening. Chip comes to work right after dinner. Usually gets here about 7:00 and works until 11:00. He does the cleaning, inventory, and the rough work in the storeroom. Say, what do you think about the zone defense?"

The stranger seemed to know all about the zone defense and all the other defenses too. He pontificated for the next hour on basketball. When he ended his discourse, Petey and Paddy were completely captivated by the glib Mr. Baxter.

T. A. K. Baxter chuckled to himself as he left the Sugar Bowl. He'd devoured three burgers, two dishes of ice cream, four cups of coffee, and a Coke. He and Petey had been so engrossed in the basketball discussion that neither seemed to notice Baxter forgot to pay his check.

After Baxter left, Petey and Paddy talked of nothing else. "He's some guy, Paddy," Petey said enthusiastically.

Paddy nodded, but his little brow was furrowed. "Why's he here?" he asked.

"Writin' a book about pottery. He's a big shot, Paddy! A real big deal! Chip'll sure be surprised about this."

Baxter was greatly pleased with himself as he swaggered back to the Inn. He always knew when he was on, and he enjoyed presenting a good performance. This afternoon he'd been at his best. Of course, he chuckled, it was literally taking candy from a baby—as well as burgers, ice cream, and coffee.

Later, Chip arrived at the Sugar Bowl and was mobbed by the brother act. Chip had never thought of Petey as an observant person, but he was surprised over how much Petey, supported by an eager Paddy, knew about the distinguished pottery authority, Mr. T. A. K. Baxter.

"Mr. Baxter played at State, Chip! *He knew your father!* He was a senior when your father was a freshman, but he played a lot of scrimmages and pickup games with him. He knows more about him than I do, and I guess I knew your dad! Chip, he's writing a book about ceramics. He'd like to meet you, and he said he'd drop in tomorrow night! He's a great guy! You'll like him, Chip.

Paddy was a junior Petey in more ways than one. Petey had shut him out so far, but when he stopped for a breath, Paddy jumped in.

"He's a great shot, Chip! Not as good as you, I bet, but he's good."

Petey had regained his breath. "Yeah," he interrupted, "he says you should shoot more three-pointers and the team should run a fast break all the time. Says it's a faster, better game. Says that you score close to the basket and that there's no reason you shouldn't shoot more of the long ones. He a terrific foul shooter too!"

Petey stopped again to catch his breath and Paddy rushed in.

"And, Chip, I bet he could be a great coach, 'cause he knows all about defenses and practicin' and scoutin' and, well, coachin'!"

Petey started again. "Yeah, Chip, he knows all about weird defenses, such as three men out in front using man-to-man defense and two men next to the basket guardin' zone style, and well, more'n I ever heard about."

Chip never said a word. He just stood there and listened to Petey and Paddy talk about a man who had really played on the same team with his father. Of course, Mr. Schroeder, Doc Jones, Rock, and lots of other people had known his father and had seen him play. But that was different from playing on the same team with someone. Even coaching an athlete was a lot different than being a teammate. Of course, Rock had been his father's coach, just as Rock was his coach, and Rock was a lot like a teammate, even though he was a pretty tough guy when it came to discipline and hard work, but it was a little different. Chip couldn't wait until tomorrow night.

CHAPTER 5

The Best Player

VALLEY FALLS high school was basketball crazy, and anyone lucky enough to make the varsity squad was envied by every student in school. Chip thought all the fuss about basketball players was nonsense and spent as little time as possible in the halls where the heroes hung out to be seen. Instead, he usually went to the gym or the athletic offices when he had a free period and could get excused. Today, he was just a bit disappointed in his English teacher, Mrs. Barker.

In the test he'd just completed, she had asked for a five-hundred-word response on the subject "Why Basketball Is an Important Extracurricular Activity"! What was getting into Mrs. Barker, anyway? Was she getting like everyone else in Valley Falls—hoop crazy? Usually she was chiefly interested in topics such as "What does Charles Dickens achieve by using a first-person character/narrator in *Great Expectations*"? Or like last month, he and Speed had put on a skit. Speed had been Hamlet, and he had been Atticus Finch. Now that had been an English *assignment!*

Chip handed in his paper and struck out for the gym. In the physical education office, Chip met Chet Stewart. With a look of relief in his face, the balding assistant coach grabbed Chip by the arm,

"The answer to my prayer! Look, Chip, hurry into the gym and help the new substitute, Barry Hauser, with this class. Prof Rogers wants me in his office right away, and the sub looks like he could use your help."

"What'll I do?"

"Just assist Mr. Hauser until I get back! You're his insurance. We're working on a basketball unit."

Stewart hurried away and Chip walked onto the gym floor. The sub, panic-stricken, looked hopefully at Chip, who was greeted by jeers from the thirty to thirty-five freshmen who were sitting on the floor, leaning back against the wall.

"Go away!"

"*Yeah,* far away!"

"Go play basketball!"

Chip laughed good-naturedly.

"That's just what we're going to do," he announced, "play basketball! We've got twenty-five minutes left and that's just enough time for two half-court games of ten minutes each. Now, I want the best eight players. You guys know who they are. Come on, step forward."

Eight boys were shoved forward, and Chip recognized Scottie Peck, Adam DeWitt, Bryan Newcomb, Shawn Todd, and one or two others. Then he noticed Brevin Barnes, a tall black student. Chip recognized Brevin as a JV player, but the two squads didn't practice together and he'd never seen him in a game. He was almost as tall as Chip but extremely slender. Brevin was still protesting to the three or four classmates who had pushed him out of the crowd. In a very few minutes the eight teams were organized, and the first games were under way.

When the bell rang, Chip enjoyed the good-natured razzing the class gave him, although he knew they were kidding around. But the feeling passed quickly, and there were two tight, little frown lines between his eyes when he walked slowly from the gym and out into the hall.

Stewart came tearing out of the opposite door and they nearly collided. "Thanks, Chip," he gasped, "thanks a lot. How'd it go?"

"Fine, Coach. Did you ever notice Brevin Barnes?"

"Sure! New this year to Valley Falls. Why?"

"Well, I just think he's going to be a great player, that's all."

Chip hesitated a second and then plunged. "He's a lot better than Scottie Peck and Adam DeWitt right now!" He watched Stewart closely; his clear gray eyes narrowed a bit and focused straight on Chet's thoughtful face.

A brief smile swept across Stewart's mouth and then he pursed his lips and nodded uncertainly. "Yes, Chip," he said thoughtfully, looking up into the solemn eyes of the tall teenager. "Maybe I can do something about that."

The tension was gone then, and the smile the two friends exchanged was deep and true. Chip turned quickly and hurried away, but Chet Stewart stood there a long minute looking down the deserted corridor, enjoying the full measure of that moment of complete understanding that all too seldom passes between coach and player. Then he turned around and headed down the hall for Rockwell's private office. He needed Rock's advice.

Coach Rockwell had been at Valley Falls from the very beginning of his coaching career. He'd seen practically every grown man in town come and go through high school, and practically every one of those men respected and admired him. To Mrs. Rockwell, he was usually Henry; to his close friends and colleagues, he was Hank; and to every athlete who had played for him and to every sports fan in town, he was Rock.

That the nickname "Rock" was fitting, everyone agreed. But to which of his attributes it best applied was a matter of varied opinion. Some thought the name was apt because of his stubborn nature; many, because of his adherence to certain iron-bound sports principles; but countless athletes and others who had visited his office for help of one kind or another knew it was appropriate because of his strength of character. Chet Stewart was one of these.

Rockwell scarcely looked up from the papers he was grading when Stewart entered. He knew the ring of Chet's footsteps well, and he knew the man who was his chief assistant and most trusted friend inside and out.

"What is it, Chet?" he asked softly.

"Er, Rock, it's about Brevin Barnes."

"Brevin Barnes?"

"New this year and made JV. He's in one of my first-year classes. And he's a good basketball player!"

"That bothers you?"

"No, but it might bother some of the other kids on the JV squad!"

"Don't get it!"

"Well, you will! You'll get it if he starts in one of the JV games in the place of DeWitt, or Peck, or Connors, or Rice, or Hill."

Rockwell suddenly straightened up in his chair and carefully placed the paper he had been reading on top of a stack of similar papers. His black eyes were alive and intent now, his thin lips were pressed tightly together, and his deliberate speech indicated he was deeply stirred.

"Chet, a coach builds up a lot of personal principles during a coaching career. Some of those we start out with develop weaknesses as we gain in experience and some improve with age. High on the list of those principles that I have found strong and right through the years I've been coaching is one that fills the bill right here. Know what it is?"

Stewart shook his head uncertainly.

"The best player gets the job!"

Stewart started to speak, but Rockwell's raised hand stopped him.

"I didn't finish, Chet," Rockwell said softly. "The best player gets the job regardless of ethnic group, creed, or family background."

There was a long silence in that little office, the kind of silence when the thoughts of two people seem to meet and convey more with greater understanding than spoken words permit. Then Stewart brushed his hand back over his thinning hair.

Rockwell's smile was one of understanding. "Chet, it's your job and my job to get the best candidates in this high school, any and all, out for the teams. Isn't it our job to put the best players on the teams? We don't ask students what church they attend. And we haven't any right, as long as an athlete is a regularly enrolled student in this school, to overlook him."

Stewart wheeled and left the room without another word, but his abrupt departure wasn't discourteous. Rockwell knew just where Stewart was going and just what he was going to do, and the little sigh that followed the sound of Chet's hurrying footsteps was one of contentment.

Rockwell knew basketball and he knew boys. He knew he had one of the strongest teams he'd ever coached. He also knew the boys knew they were good. They were confident to the point of being arrogant. One of his coaching axioms was to drill a team hard after an easy victory and easy after a defeat. That afternoon he poured it on the Big Reds because they were well rested after the Sunday layoff and because they'd won two victories in two days. He wanted them to realize two wins or six wins didn't make a successful season.

Chip was dead tired at the end of practice. After showering and changing, he started out for the Sugar Bowl. He'd been eagerly anticipating meeting T. A. K. Baxter. He kept peering out the storeroom from 7:00 until 9:00, but the stranger didn't appear. Then, from nowhere, Speed and Soapy breezed in, brimming over with additional news about the stranger.

"What a shot!" Speed said breathlessly. "Chip, he hits from everywhere!"

"He hits from downtown, Chip," Soapy exclaimed. "Nothin' but net most of the time too!"

"I heard some guys talking about him, but I didn't believe it," Speed declared excitedly. "But I believe it now! Saw it with my own eyes!"

Soapy was just as enthusiastic. "The guy just can't miss!"

"He's still there, Chip," Speed said. "Why don't you slip over for a few minutes and see for yourself. I'm going back! Come on, Soapy!"

John Schroeder, in the storeroom at his desk, looked up at the teenager he regarded almost as a son and said softly, "Of course you can go over to the Y for a few minutes, Chipper. What's up?"

Chip told him about the sharpshooting stranger; therefore, he wasn't surprised shortly after he'd reached the Y to see John Schroeder and Doc Jones come puffing into the gym.

Out on the floor, a tall man was bouncing a basketball and talking to a group of players from the Independents, one of the community teams in Valley Falls. Chip judged the man stood about six-feet-three or four. He showed the effects of an easy life by the small paunch he carried. His muscles had evidently once been long and lean and hard, but they were flabby now and Chip's opinion of the man dropped. T. A. K. Baxter might have been a player at one time, but he surely couldn't be much now.

Baxter quickly changed Chip's opinion. He moved to the free-throw line and began shooting. He buried each shot. He didn't spend much time on the shot either. Rock made players take their time, take a deep breath, and concentrate. This man simply fired the ball through the hoop as quickly as someone threw it back. Then he began to move farther away from the basket and around the three-point line. Every shot went spinning fast and true through the hoop as clean as a whistle. He was good! Maybe *great* was the word, Chip thought admiringly as he started for the steps. He turned for one last look and then glanced at his employer. John Schroeder hadn't moved. Neither had Doc Jones. Those two basketball enthusiasts sat completely absorbed in the expert marksmanship of the tall stranger.

Petey Jackson was waiting expectantly. "How is he?"

Chip nodded his head. "He's everything Speed said he was, Petey. The best I ever saw! He *never* misses!"

Petey was highly gratified. "What do you think of his long three-pointers?"

Chip cocked his head thoughtfully. "He's awesome, Petey, but remember he's not being guarded. Guess I agree with what the coach says; it seems to me a player can do most things better closer to the basket."

Chip knew Petey, and he could tell by his face that this discussion would last all night if he didn't move, so he walked back to the quiet of the storeroom and tried to do a little studying. However, thoughts of the stranger kept intruding. Finally, with a sigh, he put his books aside. Leaning back in John Schroeder's chair, he began to debate the shooting question. In a way, he was glad Soapy and Speed wouldn't be waiting for him tonight because he knew the debate would continue where Petey had left off. This was a weekday night, and Rock expected his varsity players at home and in bed by 11:00. Chip was excused because he had to work. He tried the books once again, and, at last, he could concentrate.

John Schroeder and Doc Jones came in about 10:30 just as excited as Speed and Soapy had been.

"What an exhibition!" Schroeder declared. "Why, Chip, I never saw anyone shoot like that in my life, and I've seen the Celtics and the Globetrotters and about all the great college shooters like Hank Luisetti, Pete Maravich, Jerry West, Larry Bird—well, all of them."

"You'd have to see it to believe it," Doc Jones added. "He shoots as though he has a patent on shooting!"

Fortunately for Chip, Petey chose that moment to stick his head in the door and gesture violently. "He's out front, Chip," he whispered excitedly. "Come on!"

T. A. K. Baxter had sized Chip up well, and he was smart enough to affect an air of great modesty in discussing his basketball skill. He downplayed his accuracy by offering, "Oh, anyone could learn to shoot like that if he's been at it as long as I have."

As they became better acquainted, Baxter seemingly let Chip be the one to lead him into a discussion of the Bill Hilton he'd known at State. He professed to be doubtful at first but, as he skillfully pieced the events of the "twenty or more years ago" together, he appeared to become more and more convinced that Bill Hilton was in reality Big Chip Hilton and that this teenager was Bill's son.

"What a coincidence!" he finally declared. "Who'd have believed it possible after all these years! I'll drop in tomorrow night and we'll talk some more. Looks like we've got a lot in common."

Baxter extended his hand and they exchanged firm grips. "Good night, young Chip," Baxter smiled.

Chip was thrilled. Mr. Baxter was a great guy. It sure proved you couldn't tell a person by the way he looked in a warm-up.

Chip's mother was waiting up for him when he arrived home, but that wasn't unusual. Mary Hilton never went to bed until Chip was safely home. The short half hour they spent together before bedtime was another opportunity to discuss the events of the day. And the news tonight was precious.

Mary Hilton had looked forward to hearing more about the man who'd been one of Big Chip Hilton's college friends. Chip told his mother all about Baxter's great shooting skill and about their conversation at the Sugar Bowl.

"He's very nice, Mom, and he knows all about Dad."

Mary Hilton was pleased with the news and pleased with the impression T. A. K. Baxter had made on her son. She was already planning to extend an invitation to Mr. Baxter to visit with them some evening. The thought of listening to her husband's old friend talk about his college days with Big Chip touched a chord deep in her heart.

"How long did he say he's going to be in Valley Falls, Chip?"

"He said he expects to be here a month or so researching material for a new book he's writing."

Mary Hilton's eyes sparkled. "I'll tell you what, Chip! We'll invite him to dinner next Sunday afternoon. You can ask Soapy and Speed and Biggie to come along."

"You forgot Taps."

They both laughed and were still laughing when they said good night a few minutes later. Valley Falls's six-foot-seven-inch center got his mail next door and his father, mother, and little sister lived there, but Taps spent more time at the Hiltons' than he did at home.

Tears brimmed Mary Hilton's eyes as she kissed her son good night. The years had somewhat healed her grief over Big Chip's tragic death. Now, suddenly, the gates of memory had jarred open. Out of the past had come someone who had been Big Chip's friend—someone who could share with her precious memories of Big Chip in the days when he was away at school. If only she could make Mr. Baxter's presence mean as much to her son as it meant to her.

CHAPTER 6

Misfires Abound

CHET STEWART had time for only one kind of basketball—the kind taught by the man who'd been his high school coach and who was now his boss, Henry Rockwell. Chet had heard about the great shooting of the newcomer down at the Y and was a bit disturbed by the effect the man's remarks and shooting skill was having on his JV team and on some of the varsity members. So it wasn't strange that Stewart was present at the shooting exhibition T. A. K. Baxter had been coaxed to present that night at the Y.

While Stewart sat in the bleachers watching Baxter talk to members of the Valley Falls Independents, a team made up of former high school and ex-college players, his thoughts turned to difficulties that had arisen within the past few days on his JV squad.

Baxter's influence on Valley Falls basketball wasn't all that Stewart had to worry about. He'd decided to give Brevin Barnes more playing time and had immediately run into trouble. Not that there was a rebellion of any kind among the members of the squad, but he noticed a clumsy awareness in the actions of the starting five— Scottie Peck, Adam DeWitt, Buddy Connors, Teddy Rice, and Ralph "Hillie" Hill. Chet Stewart knew enough about most of those boys and their parents to realize there were going to be some anxious minutes just as soon as Brevin Barnes began to steal the limelight away from one of the JV regulars. What's more, he knew Brevin was going to do that in the very first game he played.

The kids who made up the JV starting five represented families who might be considered Valley Falls's business and civic leaders. Teddy's father owned one of the hardware stores; Hillie's dad owned a clothing store; Adam's father was chief chemist at the pottery; and that was the way it went.

Brevin Barnes's father was a recently hired hourly worker at the pottery. Stewart groaned and almost wished he'd taken that job in the bank a few years ago when it had been offered to him. But the appearance of the tall stranger on the floor made Chet forget all about Brevin Barnes and his JV basketball problems.

Stewart had seen a lot of people shoot a basketball, but he had never seen anything like this—and neither had the fifty or sixty other basketball fans seated in the bleachers. After watching Baxter for five minutes, Chet could understand why the guy could gain and hold the admiration of Valley Falls's hoop-crazy kids and grownups. Baxter was hot! He hit from the corners, from the sides, and from deep down the middle. And every one ripped the cords. Chet whistled softly to himself. When he left the Y and walked slowly home, his mind was filled with the changes the great game of basketball had undergone in its short history.

MISFIRES ABOUND

Friday afternoon at 4:00 sharp, the school bus pulled away from the steps in front of Valley Falls High School loaded to capacity with the state basketball champions and their current season's hoop hopes. There were Prof Rogers, Coach Rockwell, Chet Stewart, Biggie Cohen, and the varsity consisting of Chip Hilton, Speed Morris, Soapy Smith, Taps Browning, Mike Rodriguez, Red Schwartz, Bill English, Ray Termini, Tim Booker, and Lefty Peters, the smallest man on the squad. Most of this group had appropriated all the front seats in the bus.

In the rear seats, there were the two JV managers and the JV reserves: Spike Davis, younger brother of Jerry Davis who was vice-president of Valley Falls's largest jewelry store and Rockwell's bitterest enemy; Ralph Knox; young Bob Blaine, the chemistry teacher's son; and one of the eleven Ferris boys. This one looked like Fred, but most all of the Ferris boys were called "Wheels," so it didn't make much difference which one it was. The JV starting five were sitting side by side, talking in muffled tones. This group was seated in the rear seat, which extended clear across the bus. Midway in the bus, in a window seat, Brevin Barnes was sitting beside Chip Hilton.

Everyone was talking and laughing and thinking about that night's game with Dane. Every once in a while, into the mind of every boy in that bus, with the exception of Biggie Cohen, Chip Hilton, and Brevin Barnes, came the thought of three-point shots.

Chet Stewart gave a thought to the shot once in a while, too, but he didn't let on to Rockwell. It was just as well, for later that night Coach Rockwell was to get a firsthand view of the impression Baxter had made on certain JV basketball players, specifically Rice, Connors,

Peck, Hill, and DeWitt. The budding Big Red JV stars lost no time in putting their three-point shooting skills into practice. As a result, at the end of the half, Dane's future greats were leading by a score of 20-9.

Rockwell saw only the first half of that game, but he watched it with an amazed expression on his face. There was a questioning look in his eyes when he studied Stewart to see what effect the wild shooting was making on his chief assistant. At the half, Rockwell went to the Big Reds' locker room to help ready his varsity. It was just as well he'd left, for the Valley Falls JVs came completely apart at the seams in the second half and absorbed a real trouncing from the jubilant Danes, 42-23.

In spite of the disappointing score, there were two Valley Falls representatives who got a kick out of that second half. Chet Stewart sent Brevin Barnes in for Ralph Hill midway in the third quarter, and Brevin proceeded to get five baskets and a free throw for a total of eleven points in exactly nine minutes.

Barnes got his points without help from his teammates. He couldn't buy a pass, but he was talented enough to use that tremendous leap of his to follow-in the Junior Big Reds' missed long shots and to tap in the rebounds. On the defense, he held Dane's big shooting gun scoreless. There was a determined slant to Chet Stewart's jaw when the game was over and he passed the varsity coming out on the floor.

Rockwell saw the 42-23 score before the scoreboard was cleared, but he said nothing to Stewart when Chet rejoined him on the bench.

Dane was up for the Big Reds. It was the only shot Dane would have at the state champs this year, and the team meant to make it interesting. They did! Taps Browning got the opening jump, and Chip came in high from his left forward position to take the ball. Red Schwartz had broken for the basket from his position, but he was covered. Chip passed the ball back to Speed Morris. Morris was the Big Reds' backcourt spark plug and usually started the plays by passing the ball ahead to Chip or Taps Browning and cutting around the post for a return pass.

This time, however, Speed surprised everyone, particularly Coach Rockwell, by attempting a long three-pointer almost from where he'd received the ball. The ball clanked off the rim. Chip and Taps were caught by surprise, and by the time they'd wheeled to rebound, the Danes had the ball and were swooping downcourt with their famed fast break for an easy score. Speed and Mike Rodriguez brought the ball upcourt, and this time it was Mike who let a long one-hander go from the right sideline. Air ball! Again the Danes broke down to their basket, clamping Speed Morris with a two-on-one play. Dane led 4-0.

Chip called time and muttered, "Hey, what's the idea?" He looking anxiously at Speed and Mike. "Come on, let's get it together."

When play resumed, it looked as though the Big Reds were going to get it together. Schwartz took Speed's pass from out of bounds under the Dane basket, dribbled fast to the frontcourt, passed to Chip, and cut around the Big Reds' captain to receive a return pass and take a wide open layup for the basket and two points. But that was the last offensive team effort for the Big Reds in the first quarter. When they gathered in front of the bench and faced an irate Rockwell, they were trailing Dane 20-12.

Rockwell's tirade, however, was to no avail. Now the three-point shooting fever had gripped everyone on the squad except Taps and Chip. Speed, Mike, Red, and even

Soapy Smith, when Rockwell sent him into the game to replace Mike Rodriguez, began firing up shots from any spot on the floor. The halftime score was 33-17.

In the locker room Rockwell was furious, and he gave them all an angry dressing down. It seemed to help when the second half began; however, by the time the fourth period rolled around, the sharpshooters were at it again. With four minutes left to play, the Big Reds were down eight points. Chip called another time, and Rockwell, in desperation, replaced Rodriguez and Schwartz with Lefty Peters and Bill English. He sent in directions for the team to attempt shots inside the three-point area *only*. That did the trick. Five quick scores by Taps and Chip enabled the Big Reds to pull the game out of the fire, 47-46.

The bus trip back to Valley Falls wasn't the ride of a victorious team—nor did things pick up when they stopped for an after-game meal halfway home. Rockwell had given them another tongue-lashing right after the game. Much as they resented the bawling out, each player knew everything Rock had said was true.

"What kind of exhibition was that? And where did you pick up that kind of shooting? And where was the team play? And what's happened to your regular shots? That question is meant for you Rodriguez, and you, Smith, and you, Schwartz.

"And where was the cutting and setting up of the plays you're supposed to be noted for, Morris? What possessed you to take those shots?

"Why didn't you try a few more hook shots, Browning? But wait. I take that back. You have to *have* the ball before you can shoot! And the only way you could have gotten that ball away from some of the members of this team tonight was by tackling them! Might have been a good idea at that! Why didn't you think of that, Hilton? You're s'posed to be—I said *supposed* to be—the captain of this team! But I didn't see any changes after your time-outs. If the captain of the team can't follow orders when they're sent in with every substitution that's made—

"State champions! Hah! Who were you trying to imitate? The JVs? What an exhibition that was! But they've got some excuse! They just don't know any better. But state champions ought to know better! State champions! Hah!"

Chip was glad to get off that bus and into the shelter of home. So was everyone else. A large airliner or a twenty-eight car train might have helped, but a twenty-eight passenger school bus was too small—much too small—when Rock was on a rampage.

Anyone looking for a hundred basketball players the next afternoon could have found them without much trouble and without much loss of time. Everyone in town knew and had known all week that Saturday afternoon Baxter was going to give another shooting exhibition. Reports came in that afternoon to Petey and Chip that the stranger had taken over the coaching of the town team and had asserted he could teach anyone to be a good shot from anywhere on the court in two weeks.

Later that afternoon, Doc Jones and John Schroeder got into one of their heated arguments about basketball. Schroeder was of the opinion that the three-pointer was pretty to watch but was a threat to team play. Doc disagreed. Chip was caught in the middle of the argument.

When asked his opinion, Chip ventured, "Guys don't like teammates who take too many shots, no matter what kind they are."

That was as far as Chip would go. His employer and Doc were still arguing when he went home to supper.

Baxter knew all about the Sugar Bowl now. He knew the rush periods and the slack ones, and he made it a point to arrive when Petey Jackson was least busy. The day before, he'd explained to Petey he was extremely forgetful about small details and if he ever forgot to pay his check to note it down and he'd settle up in a week or two. But Petey was too thoughtful to worry a great man like Baxter with such petty details, so he reached down in his own pocket or into the tips glass to cancel out the stranger's checks.

That Saturday night Baxter arrived at the Sugar Bowl right after the 9:00 rush. Before he left he'd satisfied his appetite for free and had been assured of a Sunday dinner at the Hilton home.

Later, anyone listening in on Baxter in his room would have been amazed to hear him apparently talking to Chip and Mrs. Hilton in low tones, reviewing dates and incidents that had happened years before "when Bill Hilton and I were at State."

Baxter was thorough. Whenever he planned a project, it was well thought out. Every detail was rehearsed again and again. So far, the Valley Falls pottery plan was progressing very well indeed. It seemed as though all he had to do was pull a string and the parts of his plan fell directly into place.

He'd met just about everyone of consequence in town with the exception of J. P. Ohlsen. But that was the way he wanted it. He wasn't quite ready for that meeting. The sportswriters had been easy to handle. Pete Williams of the *Post* and Joe Kennedy of the *Times* had welcomed Baxter's arrival in Valley Falls enthusiastically. Baxter's shooting had given them a basketball angle to play up, and they gave it the best they had. They went along with his pottery interest because it was wise to remember this was a pottery town first, last, and all the time. Baxter cleverly let Kennedy and Williams maneuver him into a discussion of his forthcoming book, and he talked just reluctantly enough to encourage them to expand on the information he gave so grudgingly concerning his personal business.

That night, when T. A. K. Baxter tucked his slowly shrinking roll of bills into his sock and then under his pillow, he felt highly gratified with his progress. Tomorrow he'd get one foot inside the door of the Hilton home at Sunday afternoon dinner. Then things would really start to move.

CHAPTER 7

Storm Signals

MRS. HILTON, Mrs. Browning, Taps, and his sister, Suzy, were bustling around the kitchen. Chip, making himself scarce, went into the living room to read the papers. He turned immediately to the sports page of the *Times* and read Joe Kennedy's "Times and Sports." Although Chip was one of Kennedy's most consistent readers, what he read this Sunday morning brought a furrow to his forehead.

Times and Sports
by Joe Kennedy

The Dane game. What happened? Should have been won by twenty instead of one. Credit for victory solely due to stretch play of Hilton and Browning. Hilton held to 14 points . . . maybe that's the reason.

And what about the JV team, which is supposed to be crammed full of varsity talent?

STORM SIGNALS

The pottery convention and exhibit is over, but Valley Falls's basketball fans are learning more basketball than pottery from T. A. K. Baxter, noted chemist, who has chosen Valley Falls as a working location to complete his newest book on modern ceramics.

The shooting controversy is raging all over town. John Schroeder and Doc Jones are, as usual, on opposite sides of the fence.

Brevin Barnes, newcomer to Valley Falls this year, got in the JV game at Dane and scored a neat eleven points in nine minutes. Mean anything to you, Rock?

Could it be the Big Reds' drive is suffering because of Chip Hilton's high scoring? This reporter thought certain members of the team passed him up regularly for their own three-point attempts.

Stratford this coming Saturday. That's the last of the easy ones. Ten tough ones in a row after that—all willing and several of them capable of dousing the Big Reds' championship repeat hopes.

Valley Falls Independents play the Steeltown Crescents Christmas Day at 4:00 at the high school gym. Good game and a good cause . . . Hospital Fund. See you there.

Chip finished the column, tossed the paper on the sofa, and descended to the lab in the basement. He was still there when Speed, Soapy, Biggie, and Taps came clattering down the steps. Biggie and Taps were as much interested in the meal to come as in the personal appearance at the Hilton home of the noted stranger, T. A. K. Baxter. But not Speed and Soapy. Speed could hardly wait for Baxter to arrive, showing his excitement by restlessly squirming and talking about Christmas and the holidays and the game, while Soapy digressed nervously on the "small change" stories Kennedy and Williams had printed about the Dane game.

Finally the great man came swinging jauntily along and onto the front porch. He already knew the boys and captivated Mrs. Hilton and Mrs. Browning almost with his first words, but Chip noticed Suzy's scrunched-up nose and folded arms as she listened to Baxter's stories. Baxter entertained everyone with his basketball experiences. The stories were cleverly told and enthralled his listeners. Naturally, he was in the starring role in most of the games he described, but he was clever enough to leave most of that to the boys' imaginations.

After dinner, sitting in the living room with Mary Hilton and Karen Browning while the boys and Suzy were cleaning up the kitchen, Baxter really turned on the charm.

Yes, he liked Valley Falls very much. Naturally his chief interest was pottery, but he liked sports in general and basketball in particular because he'd played the game so much in college. His book would keep him here for at least a month. Yes, living in the Inn was lonely, but it was quiet and it wouldn't be too bad, he guessed . . .

Baxter cleverly guided and kept the conversation on pottery. He talked about Bill Hilton's study of ceramics at State and referred to a number of experiments they'd worked out together. Then, just as if he had pulled another string, Mary Hilton asked him if he'd like to see Bill's small laboratory. Baxter could scarcely conceal his eagerness, but in a casual tone he said yes, he'd be delighted.

Chip had never been too keen about anyone inspecting his father's lab. Several times Mrs. Hilton had to use her greatest diplomacy to cover up Chip's obvious annoyance while they were talking and puttering around the room. But Baxter noticed nothing out of the way, apparently. His quick eyes swept around the room, noting in one comprehensive glance the gas-fired kiln, the mixer, the wheel, the sink, and the jars of finely ground feldspar, soapstone, quartz, and kaolin as well as clays of every color. The locked filing cabinet drew his attention, but he made no reference to its contents.

Before they went upstairs, however, he brought up the subject of formulas, and Mary Hilton fell right into the trap.

"Oh, don't say formulas to me. There used to be hundreds of them scattered all over the house, until I threatened to burn them. Then Chip bought that old filing cabinet over there, and now they're all safely locked away."

Chip shuffled his feet uneasily, and again Mrs. Hilton tried to ease the situation. "Don't mind Chip if he appears annoyed, Mr. Baxter. He never allows anyone down here and keeps the door locked as if it were Fort Knox."

Later, upstairs in the living room, Chip covertly watched the stranger talking to his mother. Why couldn't he like this man? His deportment was perfect, but something was wrong. There was something—something he couldn't explain, even to himself.

Before leaving, Baxter told Mrs. Hilton he intended to list some of Bill Hilton's formulas in the book and give him the credit he deserved but had never received. That was the clincher! Mrs. Hilton was overcome. Then and there she decided to invite Baxter to Christmas dinner.

Baxter said it was an imposition, but he gracefully consented to come because he knew she was influenced by her Christian spirit. Christmas was an empty period in his life because he'd never married and his parents were no longer living. He was honored and grateful for the privilege of sharing the holiday in her home.

That night Chip couldn't get to sleep. After a long discussion, he and his mom had agreed to ask Mr. Baxter to move into their home for the month or two he'd be in Valley Falls. Chip hadn't been keen about it and had tried several excuses: "It'll be added work and a lot of trouble."

But Mary Hilton had overcome his objections. Mrs. Browning would come over and take care of his room and make coffee for him every morning. Besides, the house was too large for just the two of them; it was the holidays; and most important, Baxter was one of his father's friends.

More than everything else, Chip wanted his mother to be happy. He wasn't home very much in the evenings, and it would be nice to have someone in the house to keep her company until he got home.

Then the team and the Dane game occupied his thoughts, and he forgot Baxter completely in his attempts to figure out the changes taking place in the team. What had happened to Mike Rodriguez? Mike was one of the best shooters from eight to twelve feet, and here he was taking long, crazy shots. All the other guys were trying them too. That brought Chip's thoughts back to the stranger and his three-point shooting. Chip had a hunch that it all meant trouble. It was with that thought that at last he fell into a restless, uneasy sleep.

Baxter had no trouble getting to sleep that night. He knew he'd made real progress. He hadn't missed the quick expression of sympathetic understanding that swept over Mrs. Hilton's face when he said the Inn was a bit lonely. Then she'd invited him for Christmas dinner. He knew that on that day, just as if he pulled another string, she'd ask him to move into the Hilton home for the duration of his stay in Valley Falls. He smiled to himself in satisfaction.

Everything would be perfect then. Mary Hilton worked all day, and the kid was at school. He'd be alone with plenty of time to get into the lab and that filing cabinet. Then he'd be ready for J. P. Ohlsen.

But he'd have to be careful about that kid. The boy didn't like the idea of anyone messing around in the lab. Baxter'd have to play it smart. The kid was more than just a high school athlete. He was nobody's fool, and his suspicions might easily be aroused.

CHAPTER 8

Regulars Benched

CHIP WANTED to sleep late the next day, the first day of the two-week Christmas vacation. There would be no school until Thursday, January 2. Habit was too strong, however, and he was up as usual before his mother left for work. When he closed his window, he had a surprise. Valley Falls's first real snow had fallen, and a white Christmas looked promising.

Chip spent the hour after his mother left shoveling snow off the sidewalk and puttering around the house. He then hurried down to the Sugar Bowl and repeated the performance.

As Chip worked, his thoughts shifted from one thing to another. First, he thought of Baxter, the man who knew so much about his father. Then he thought about the team and the crazy shooting that seemed to have become almost a disease with every basketball player in town. His thoughts shifted to Brevin Barnes, and he felt good because Brevin had made such a good showing in the Dane game.

REGULARS BENCHED

Chip chuckled when be thought of the compliments Brevin had received in Williams's and Kennedy's columns. That probably was the first time Barnes had ever seen his name in the paper. But it wouldn't be the last time. Then Chip thought of their plans to practice at the Y every morning. Ty Higgins, the director, always let Chip practice at the gym when it wasn't in use, and he'd said, "Sure, it's all right to bring a friend." Therefore Chip and Brevin had decided to practice every morning at 9:00 during the holidays.

Chip was puffing a bit now as he tried to force his thoughts to keep pace with his shoveling, so he stopped to rest and catch his breath. He began to concentrate on the things he planned to teach the eager freshman.

He'd have to work on Brevin's defense most of all. The boy didn't know how to keep his weight back so he could move as quickly as his opponent. Also, Brevin turned his head away from his man all the time. That was no good. Every good basketball player knows the time to cut against a guard is when he turns his head. Brevin would have to learn to use peripheral vision, to look straight ahead but sideways at the same time.

As if to demonstrate to himself, Chip leaned the shovel against his leg and stretched his arms out straight to his sides. Looking straight ahead, he wiggled his fingers and moved his arms farther and farther back until they were directly in line with his shoulders. Just as Rock said, he could see them just as well looking straight ahead, if he concentrated.

During the holidays, Rockwell called practice at the usual time. There was no changing the Rock. Practice was practice, and if you didn't want to practice, then you didn't want to play! However, on Tuesday Coach grudgingly announced the next practice would be held at the regular time Thursday.

Suddenly Christmas was gone and Baxter moved in. He was careful to let everyone know it meant a great deal to him to dwell in the home where his friend Bill Hilton had once lived. He turned on the charm for all the people he met, especially for Chip Hilton's pals.

The Valley Falls Independents played the Steeltown Crescents at the high school Christmas Day and won by a score of 103-81. It was the greatest number of points the Independents had ever scored in a single game. In fact, it was the greatest number of points any Valley Falls team had ever scored, and it made Coach Baxter. Everyone raved about the high scoring, the constant fast-break action, and the three-point prowess of the locals.

"Every starting-five player scored double figures!"

"Think of it! One hundred and three points!"

Only a few observers recognized that the Crescents had also scored a lot of points. But these few were real basketball fans who liked the game for its all-round play, balance between offense and defense, clever passing, development and execution of sound plays and, above all, teamwork.

Practice the day before the Stratford game, Friday, December 27, was the worst of the year. Chet Stewart's JVs had practiced from 1:00 to 3:00, and Chet came into Rockwell's office a short time later, mumbling something about "crazy basketball and crazier half-wits who teach kids a lot of crazy stuff!"

Rockwell usually got a kick out of Stewart's bulling, but there was no humor in his eyes today. "Now what?" he asked quietly.

Stewart slouched down in the chair opposite Rockwell's

desk. "I have just been advised what's wrong with the kind of basketball we're trying to teach!" he said viciously.

"That's interesting," Rockwell observed dryly. "Which self-proclaimed coach is it now? Jerry Davis or Doc Jones?"

"Oh, it's none of the local crew. You've probably heard of the new coaching genius in town? The great Baxter? Well, today guess who shows up at practice? That's right! The president of the 'National Federation for the Development of the Long Fire-It-at-the-Hoop and Fast Break Association of Basketball!' Yep, that's who it was!

"He came to practice, if you please, at the invitation of Teddy Rice, Ralph Hill, and Spike Davis. It seems that the Chamber of Commerce, Lions Club, Rotarians, Kiwanians, and some others enjoyed the presence of a guy named Baxter a couple of days ago at their joint luncheon, and he informed them that his chief hobby in life is kids and basketball.

"Then he proved it by spending a morning with their kids at the Y. And today he honored me with his personal appearance at our practice."

"And?"

"And after he was properly introduced, of course, by the youngest member of the family in town who gives you and me the most adverse publicity—the Davis family—he proceeds to tell me we're way behind the times in our basketball principles. That our offense is no longer practical because and because and because and . . . indefinitely!"

Rockwell stirred in his chair and glanced at the clock on the wall. "Time for practice," he said softly. "We'd better get out on the floor before someone like old Muddy Waters or Tom Brasher moves in and really shows us how to coach." Rockwell and Stewart erupted into loud laughter until a wheezing Rockwell declared, "Let's go!"

Chip sensed something was up the minute Rockwell's whistle shrilled. He knew it the second they were seated in the bleachers and he saw the board. When the Rock stopped tossing the marker in the air, Chip knew there was an important session coming.

"Basketball is first, last, and all the time *a team game*! No team ever went far against good competition just because it was composed of five great shooters, or because it had five great guards, or five great passers.

"Last year this team won the state championship because it was composed of kids who played as a team. There were no individual stars and no great scorers. This year we have every one of those boys back with the exception of the Scott brothers. And as a substitute for those two, we have our captain, Chip Hilton.

"We're a good team! Maybe a great team! Maybe we're good enough to repeat as state champions. But we're never going to do that playing the way we've been playing and practicing the past two weeks. We barely scraped past Dane, and we've looked pretty bad in practice ever since.

"Now I've been in basketball as a player and as a coach a long time. I've seen good players and good teams come and go. I'll probably see more. But I never saw a team win a championship unless its players pulled together and played as a team.

"There's one more important item. Few great teams got that way without someone to lead and guide them. Someone has to take the responsibility for the coaching and the leadership. The coaching is my responsibility. You elected your own leader, Chip Hilton.

"As the coach, it's my job to get you and keep you in shape, to outline a style of play offensively and defensively, to place the best players in the various positions and to keep them there unless they prove detrimental to the team, to scout the opposition, to use all the experience at my command to assist you to win games, and to teach you to play hard and play to win, and to show by my deportment and language that I can be a modest winner and a gracious loser.

"It's my job to maintain and teach discipline, team spirit, and team play, and I'm going to do it! Now I'm fully aware everyone likes to see his name in the papers, likes to score, and likes to play an important part in his team's success. But I'm also aware it isn't possible for every player on a team to take the leading part in every game, for there aren't enough leading parts. Someone has to be the feeder, someone has to be the driver, someone has to set up the plays, someone has to be the stalwart on the defense, and someone has to get the most points.

"The way you've been playing lately, it's clear each of you wants to make the points. All the points! And you want to make them the hard way—as far away from the basket as possible! What's more, you'll take as many shots as you can get to do it!"

Rockwell quickly sketched the outline of half a court. Then he drew three curved lines extending from each sideline.

Tapping the board to accentuate his words, he continued, "This is the way you're going to play from now on. Under the basket, I expect you to swing your shoulders around and square-up to the basket before you release the shot and bank the ball off the backboard.

"Between this bank-shot area and the line extending from just inside the corners to the back of the free-throw circle, I want smooth jump shots—shots with the shoulders squared to the basket, just as they're squared in the bank-shot area.

"In the third area, in the three-point area, you'll use fewer attempts—and *only* as part of our planned offense. The first player who attempts a wild shot from this area will be benched! Is that clear?"

Rockwell paused and searched each player's eyes. Then he continued in a milder voice, "Now, let's have a short workout and try to look like the team that won the state championship!"

Practice was short and terrible. There was no drive, no pep, no desire to play. Rockwell sighed and sent the team to the showers.

Not much was said by the guys in Speed's Mustang as the car slid slowly along Main Street, but when they reached the Sugar Bowl and were sitting in the middle of the high school crowd at the soda fountain, Soapy said flippantly, "Rock was in pretty good form this afternoon, wasn't he?"

"We had it coming!" Chip retorted flatly.

"Maybe," Speed responded thoughtfully. "Maybe we did and maybe we didn't! I just don't understand why he's getting all bothered about three-pointers."

In the debate that followed, Petey Jackson was an interested listener for a short time. Finally he had to jump in. "Seems to me the Independents are doin' all right with three's and fast breaks," he said aggressively. "Maybe Rock is a little jealous of any kind of basketball 'cept what he teaches."

Chip lowered himself slowly from the fountain stool. "Could be," he said quietly, "but I seem to remember a shot that won the state championship for Valley Falls last year! Whose kind of basketball was that?" Then he abruptly turned around and walked back to the storeroom.

REGULARS BENCHED

Chip and Brevin practiced at the Y for an hour the next morning. Chip was pleased with Brevin's progress. The slender freshman was fast on his feet and quick to learn. Once he was told about a certain pass or shot, it wasn't necessary to drum it into him. He was a natural.

The Valley Falls junior varsity starting five had played for West Side Middle School as a team and were intact as freshmen. Now, almost ready for varsity duty, they were complacently looking forward to next year when the varsity would lose Hilton, Morris, Schwartz, Rodriguez, and Smith. Then it would be their turn. Of course, Taps Browning, Lefty Peters, and Bill English would be back, but they were more or less varsity reserves now, with the exception of Browning. Certainly Rockwell wasn't the kind of guy to break up an experienced team like they'd be.

Peck, DeWitt, Connors, Rice, and Hill were so busy thinking about next year as they all sat dressed for the game in the locker room that they never even caught Chet Stewart's first words. But when they heard, ". . . and Barnes at right guard," their heads jerked up in shocked surprise.

When they turned to look at Ralph Hill, he was staring at Stewart with his mouth half open, as if he didn't believe his ears. Barnes at right guard? That was Hillie's spot! Was Chet kidding? What was eating Stewart now? Barnes a regular? On the starting five? Well, he'd soon find out that starting and staying in there were two different things!

So Ralph Hill, a regular member of the JV starting five, sat on the bench when the JV game with Stratford began, still wondering if it was true. A lot of Valley Falls basketball fans who liked to see the Little Reds start off the evening's program also sat there hardly believing it was true.

Up in the stands, Ralph Hill Sr., owner of the leading clothing store in town, half rose to his feet, then sat down mumbling something. He joined Mrs. Hill in looking from their son sitting on the bench to Brevin Barnes out on the floor then back to the determined face of the JV basketball coach.

Several people looked at Hillie's parents, sitting there tense and pale, and there was a lot of whispering.

"A black player in Ralph Hill's place?"

"There's going to be a lot of trouble about this!"

"What do they need him for?"

"I wouldn't want to be in Stewart's shoes when this game's over."

"Nor Rockwell's. He's responsible! He's in charge!"

"That kid better be good!"

No one had to worry about that part of it. Brevin Barnes was the best player on the floor, scoring eighteen points. Still, there was a lot of head shaking and frowning from many of the fans. The Little Reds easily defeated Stratford, and Ralph Hill got in for most of the game—but not in the place of Brevin Barnes.

Chet Stewart kept Barnes in for the full game. One by one the previous regulars replaced each other in the line-up. As each change was made, another family became incensed because of Chet Stewart's unbelievable action of inserting Barnes on a team that not only had played together for three years but was composed of players representing the *best* families in town.

The varsity game was anticlimactic. Everyone was talking about the JV game, and the failure of the fans to cheer and lift the Big Reds out of their doldrums was nearly responsible for the first defeat of the season.

REGULARS BENCHED

Stratford was supposed to be a pushover, but it was a tough game every second of the way. The Big Reds still showed the effects of the week of desultory practice. Mike Rodriguez, Speed Morris, Red Schwartz, and Soapy Smith were still sold on firing up the ball and tried every time they got a chance.

At the start of the second half, Rockwell benched Mike and Red, replacing them with Lefty Peters and Soapy Smith. A little later when Soapy tried a wild shot, Bill English came in to relieve him.

Chip had never felt more out of a game in his life. He and Taps received the ball only when their teammates' shots were impossible. Consequently, the attack bogged down. It was sheer personal ability that enabled the Big Reds to stagger through to win, 44-40. Chip managed to get twelve points, making him the high scorer for the Big Reds.

Despite two victories, the crowd filing out of Ohlsen Gym wasn't the usual happy, cheering, and laughing crowd. It was a low-murmuring, whispering crowd, puzzled and confused about a lot of things.

The crew of basketball champions who piled into the Morris fastback were a quiet, thoughtful crowd too. When Chip swung out of the car in front of the Sugar Bowl, he was almost glad to get away from the tense atmosphere gripping his friends. He was glad to get to work cleaning and closing up and glad to be walking home alone over the hard-packed snow, even though it made the short walk a long, lonely one.

When he got home and found Baxter, Mr. and Mrs. Browning, and his mom waiting, he was glad for the first time in a long while to hurry away to bed. Later, lying there in the dark, Chip Hilton was a hurt, sad teenager. Suddenly he almost hated T. A. K. Baxter for what he was doing to the team, to his friends, and to the town.

CHAPTER 9

The Starting Five

T. A. K. BAXTER was clever with people and with locks. The lock on the lab door had been easy, but the lock on the filing cabinet containing Bill Hilton's formulas had stopped the sharpshooting locksmith cold—but not for long. After several unsuccessful attempts, he'd solved that problem by taking the number of the filing cabinet and writing directly to the manufacturer. He was careful to request that the key be mailed to his post office box.

The key had come through promptly, and Baxter's plan was working out according to schedule. There was only one hitch—Mrs. Browning. Anxious to take good care of her neighbor's guest, she blundered into the house without warning at all times of the day. That meant he'd have to time his visits to the lab just right. Then, too, he'd have to be extremely careful to leave everything just as he'd found it.

Baxter had tried working in the lab but had decided it was too dangerous. Now, each morning he brought the formulas to his room, one at a time, and replaced them each afternoon.

Everything was progressing very well. His meals were provided by Mrs. Browning and Mary Hilton and, of course, the Sugar Bowl, where he could maneuver a snack from Petey Jackson in exchange for a bit of basketball lore. Ever since he'd assumed the coaching responsibilities of the Valley Falls Independents and his run-and-gun basketball had clicked with Valley Falls's hoop fans, Petey Jackson had been completely in his power.

The Sunday sports pages featured a number of stories about the Stratford games as well as the progress the Independents were making. Kennedy's column in the *Times* and Williams's story in the *Post* made several references to the future of a new junior varsity star by the name of Brevin Barnes.

Baxter was sitting in the Hilton living room early that Sunday morning reading Kennedy's "Times and Sports" when Chip came down to breakfast. "Come here, Chip. Look at this column of Kennedy's! Sorta got you fellows on the hot seat."

Chip reluctantly took the paper and sat down on the wing chair. The first few lines were enough to put him on his guard. Baxter's mouth twisted in a smirk of satisfaction as he fingered his small mustache and watched Chip's reaction to Joe Kennedy's story.

Times and Sports
by Joe Kennedy

Last night's basketball game between Valley Falls and Stratford brought back memories of last year's state championship basketball team.

What's happened to the smooth play that carried last year's Big Reds from an underdog role to highest honors as the best team in the state? How can a team—a veteran team—lose its form so completely?

Brevin Barnes, the new basketball star on Valley Falls's sports horizon, stole all scoring honors for both games last night when he scored eighteen points. Chip Hilton was held to only twelve points.

Stratford nearly did what some Section Two rival is going to do any day now. The Big Reds are coming apart at the seams as surely as the Little Reds' Brevin Barnes is one of the greatest basketball prospects ever to break into the basketball picture at Valley Falls as a freshman. Yes, that's right, a freshman.

Watching the play of some of Hank Rockwell's varsity stars last night, I noticed Brevin Barnes is playing better ball right now than two and possibly three members of Rock's state championship team.

Have you been watching the scores the Valley Falls Independents have been running up? Rockwell's Big Reds could use a few more points. Can it be that Rock's antipathy to the three-pointers and the fast break, employed so effectively by the Independents, is responsible for the sagging defense opponents always employ against the Big Reds? A long three often opens up a sagging defense. Sure, everyone knows that Chip Hilton and Taps Browning, leading scorers of the Big Reds, score practically all their points within fifteen feet of the basket. Still, it seems the Big Reds could benefit from Hilton's dropping back into three-point territory—he's almost there anyway. With that great percentage of his—well, do the math.

By the way, Brevin Barnes has definitely shelved one of the Little Reds' veterans. And this writer

received a number of bitter letters in the mail this past
week concerning the use of Barnes in the Dane game.

I wonder if any of you anonymous writers saw
the game last night? Probably wouldn't mean anything to you anyway. If you can't sign your name to a
letter, you probably can't add. So, I'll do the math for
you: Barnes scored eleven points at Dane and eighteen last night against Stratford, and that makes a total
of twenty-nine. Is the varsity calling?

Chip shook his head slowly as he finished reading
the column. The article meant more trouble. The gap
that had opened from nowhere in his friendship with
Speed, Soapy, Red, and Mike because of his dislike for
the wild shots and lack of team play and because of his
interest in Brevin Barnes would probably grow wider.

Chip was right about the tension that had crept into
his friendships. It was evidenced in the practices and at
the Sugar Bowl. It was an uncomfortable situation, but
there was no way to get at it without coming right out
with a direct question. However that seemed foolish
since there'd been no open break of any kind.

Chip knew some of his friends resented his practices
with Brevin Barnes at the Y each morning, but he wasn't
going to stop—not when Brevin showed such a burning
desire to become a good player.

Before it seemed possible, Thursday, January 2—the
first day of school following vacation—arrived and Chip
was back in the routine of school, practice, work, and
studying. His mind was so busy he didn't have time to
worry about the situation.

Coach Rockwell was busy, too, but not too busy to
worry about several annoying matters. First on the list

was his team and the game with Dulane the following night. Maybe it was the way the practices had been going, and maybe it was the undercurrent he'd sensed in the boys, but he had a hunch that the Dulane game meant trouble. Dulane was admittedly weak and had lost to Clinton, the team Valley Falls had swamped a month ago. But the Big Reds weren't the team they'd been then.

There were a couple of other matters that had upset Rockwell this morning. Here it was, the very first school day of the year, with New Year's resolutions little more than a day old, and certain petty people were writing him letters and calling him on the phone about something that was none of their business.

Ever since the past football season, when there had been such a big fiasco about the coaching staff, the animosity between himself and a few of the younger sports fans in town had been acute. For the past two weeks these same troublemakers had aired their feelings about Brevin Barnes to such an extent that Rockwell had found it necessary to tell them to mind their own business.

But this morning some of the older and more stable residents of Valley Falls had telephoned regarding Barnes. First it had been George Connors who called and lamely suggested Stewart use Barnes as a sub rather than as a starter. "The kids have been playing together so long, Rock. It seems a shame to break up the team."

Then Jim Rice had called—big, boisterous, happy-go-lucky Jim Rice, wealthy owner of Valley Falls's major hardware store. "Hi ya, Rock! Er . . . Happy New Year to you and the family! Say, what's this Teddy tells me about Chet Stewart throwing Ralph Hill off the JVs for a new kid!"

And then, when another call came in from J. H. Davis, president of Valley Falls Jewelry, the coincidence was too much. The whole thing was a setup, Rockwell decided, and the pressure just short of being antagonistic. He held to his principles and explained his position much as he'd explained it to Chet Stewart and suggested to each caller that the issue could probably be discussed more intelligently in a personal meeting. He assured each caller, too, that he'd be glad to meet anytime to talk it over.

Rockwell sighed wearily and started on the pile of letters that had accumulated over the vacation. He came to a letter postmarked Tuesday, December 31. He read it slowly and thoughtfully, and when he'd finished, he leaned back in his chair, suddenly tired and discouraged. The letter he'd just read disturbed him more than all the phone calls, wild shots, wanna-be coaches, and challenges of coaching a state championship team put together. He looked at the signatures. Yes, they'd all signed it—all except Ralph Hill.

Just then the phone rang again and Rockwell reluctantly answered. This time it was Bob Blaine, head of the high school chemistry department and one of Rockwell's best friends. Rock, holding his breath, waited for Blaine to begin. Surely Bob wouldn't give him the same line he'd been listening to all morning.

"Hank, Bobby told me something about the difficulties Stewart's been experiencing with the JVs and also something about a letter. Have you received it? Just reading it? Well, Hank, I'd just like you to know Bobby told me last night he's a little ashamed of his part in that letter and, well, I guess you know better than I do how it is with kids and how they stick together no matter how they feel inside. And, Hank, if I can help in any way . . ."

Rockwell felt a little better when he said good-bye to Blaine, but when he returned to the letter and reread the scrawled words, his chin line slackened again and his eyes were deeply troubled.

Dear Coach Rockwell:

We know you know about Brevin Barnes
taking Hillie's place on the team and we
hate to bother you, but we know you don't
like to see a winning combination broken
up and we'd like to ask you to ask Chet
Stewart to put Hillie back on the starting
five and use Brevin as the sixth man. We
like Brevin all right, but we play better
with Hillie.

Yours truly,

Spike Davis   Scottie Rock
Fred Ferris   Adam DeWitt
Bob Knox   Buddy Connors
Bob Blaine   Selby Rice

Coach Rockwell made up his mind to attend that afternoon's Little Reds' practice session.

Nine of the ten players reporting that afternoon for
JV basketball practice were extremely nervous. The
usual locker room chatter and horseplay were strangely
missing. Each of the nine felt a little guilty, as if he'd
done something wrong and, in spite of himself, glanced
two or three times at Brevin Barnes dressing quietly in
the corner. Each one wanted to say something to Brevin,
but the words wouldn't come. Anyway, the other guys
were there, and what could a guy say?

THE STARTING FIVE

The tenth team member, Brevin Barnes, felt the unusual quietness too. Nonetheless, he went on with his dressing, more concerned about basketball than anything in the world right then. Suddenly, however, the room became so still you could have heard a whisper. Barnes looked up to see Coach Henry Rockwell standing in the doorway.

Rockwell's black eyes were friendly, and his thin lips were slanted in that crooked little smile that every boy there knew. Suddenly, everything seemed all right again.

"Hello, men," Rockwell said softly. "Coach Stewart will be along in a few minutes. In the meantime, I'd like to have a little chat with some of you. Bob—"

Two heads jerked up and two pairs of startled eyes flashed wide open. But Rockwell was looking directly at young Bob Blaine, so Bob Knox slumped back down in his seat like a limp rag.

"Bob," Rockwell continued, "suppose you and Brevin go out and shoot a few baskets. The rest of us will be out in a minute or two."

Rockwell knew boys and liked boys; he particularly liked this group. What's more, the boys in that room knew and liked the Rock too. But now, as they waited, the eyes that were focused so intently on Rockwell's face were just a bit wary, just a bit worried. It was about the letter all right . . . it had to be the letter.

When Bob Blaine and Brevin Barnes were gone, Rockwell closed the door and pulled the letter out of his pocket. When Ralph Hill said he hadn't seen the letter, Rockwell read it all the way through and then read the names. After a short pause, he began to talk, using straight-from-the-shoulder terms, pulling no punches.

Rockwell told them what he'd told Chet Stewart, except he explained it more carefully. As he talked, the strain disappeared from those tense young faces, and a light of understanding flickered in their eyes. He told them there was no such thing as a "five-man" team. The *thump, thump, thump* from the gym floor above and the exultant shouts of joy attesting to successful shots brought those eight heads up. Suddenly eight hopeful All-Americans understood what Coach Rockwell was talking about.

When the boys left the locker room to join Bob Blaine and Brevin Barnes for practice, the Little Reds' starting five was history. Chet Stewart had himself a *team*!

On Friday, January 3, the slim crowd watching the Little Reds warm up for their battle with Dulane's JVs was back to normal. The old regulars were there of course. There were a few of the kids' friends as well as George and Gerrie Connors, Big Jim and Leslie Rice, Ralph and Megan Hill, Jerry Davis, and Bob Blaine. Practically all the older spectators were especially anxious to see what Hank Rockwell was going to do about the ridiculous situation Chet Stewart had been stupid enough to fall into. They looked curiously at Stewart to see if they could figure out how he felt about all the trouble he'd caused.

Ralph and Megan Hill were particularly interested observers because Hillie had acted strangely last night at the dinner table when they'd asked him about practice. Each was thinking how difficult it was to understand teenagers nowadays, especially when you did everything in the world for them—like fighting to keep them on the team and spending hours of time every day planning things for them that they never seemed to appreciate.

Broad smiles spread across his parents' faces when, just before the game began, Hillie took off his jacket and tossed it on the bench. Two rows ahead of them Jim Rice swung around, nodded at Ralph, and winked knowingly.

But when big, happy-go-lucky Jim Rice turned back to look at the starting five, the smile froze on his face. Brevin Barnes was standing there without his jacket, and in the little circle, gripping hands with Coach Stewart, were Scottie Peck, Adam DeWitt, Buddy Connors, and Hillie Hill.

Jim Rice's face flushed a deep purple, and he smothered an oath as his wife's sharp elbow poked him in the ribs.

"What's the matter with Teddy, Jim?" she whispered. "He isn't on the starting five! Do you suppose he's sick?"

Just then, just as if he'd heard her words, Teddy Rice turned and smiled at his father and mother. There was an impish grin on the face of the captain of the Little Reds as he noted the sour expressions on his parents' faces.

Then the game was on, and the spectators sat amazed at what they saw. The Little Reds were playing the best basketball of their careers! The amazing part of it was the way they were whipping the ball to their tall, slender, lightning-fast teammate and the way they slapped him on the back or high-fived him when he scored. A little later, when the observers looked at the bench, Henry Rockwell was sitting there watching the Little Reds as intently as if he were the JV coach.

Just as Jim Rice made up his mind to go down and have a showdown with Henry Rockwell, Teddy Rice stood up, pulled off his jacket, ran to the scorer's table, and reported. Already showing signs he was going to be a big, happy-go-lucky guy like his father, Teddy kneeled down in front of the table and grinned across the floor at his parents with an impish gleam in his eyes that his mother could see all that distance away.

Jim Rice breathed heavily. It was a good thing Rockwell had come along in time to stop this nonsense. Guess that was the reason he was on the bench. What was the matter with that Stewart?

Brevin Barnes scored and Teddy trotted out on the floor. Adam DeWitt said something to Teddy and then stopped long enough to slap Brevin Barnes on the back before he trotted off the floor. Once again, certain adults who never missed a JV game looked at one another in amazement.

Before they realized it, the game was over, and they saw their kids pounding a tall newcomer on the back. They didn't know Brevin Barnes had just scored twenty-seven points. In fact, they didn't even know the final score of the game. They did know, however, that their kids seemed unusually happy and proud about winning a basketball game.

Some of the adults who'd sat there through the game felt as though they'd just received a lecture or had been to church, almost as though the kids had been teaching them something.

Some of those same adults understood what it was all about. They knew the score. Yet there were others who didn't quite get it, and they were still trying to figure it out when the Big Reds came dashing out on the floor.

CHAPTER 10

Sick at Heart

SCOUTING IS just as important to the success of a high school basketball team as it is to a major league baseball or college football team. In basketball, scouting plays an important part because a good scout can prepare his team to meet particular or peculiar defenses and help them build up a defense for the opponents' style of attack. In addition, the expert basketball scout can carry back to his team important information concerning the other team's individual players.

Coach Henry Rockwell liked to do his own scouting whenever possible. However, high school games in Section Two were usually played on Friday or Saturday nights. Because the Big Reds were usually playing the same night, he often had to rely upon hearsay, past experience, or upon a report tendered by some interested member of the alumni.

There had been no scouting reports on Dulane, and now, as Rockwell sat on the bench and watched the visitors' one-three-one zone completely bottle up the Big Reds' attack, he mentally kicked himself for not sending someone to check Dulane's current attack and defense. He looked at the scoreboard. What he saw snapped him into action. The clock showed only five minutes remaining in the first half with Dulane leading, 17-9.

Rockwell concentrated on the defense the tall visitors were using. His quick black eyes noted the slides that the passing of the ball by an attacking team always forces. Such slides are usually the tip-off to the weaknesses of any zone. It was then that Rockwell noted, for the first time, that the Big Reds were not whipping the ball around the way a good team whips it around against a zone defense.

It wasn't long before he knew why. Rodriguez, Morris, and Schwartz were banging away with wild jump-shot attempts at every opportunity. The shots were legitimate according to the chart he'd outlined for game shooting, but they weren't wise shots. The attempts usually came after a short dribble and from forced and awkward positions. Rockwell waited until Dulane scored again. Then he abruptly stood up, waited until Chip saw him, and called, "Time!"

Rockwell barked, "Start passing that ball around the way you're supposed to be doing. Chip, try a two-one-two attack; the two-two-one won't work!

"Morris, you and Schwartz handle the ball in the backcourt, and Chip, you and Mike take the corners and the sides. Taps, you work across the court from side to side near the free-throw line. Now when someone takes a shot, and I hope it'll be a good shot for a change, I want Chip, Mike, and Taps, to follow-in every time!

"Come on, now, let's play a little basketball!"

Rockwell had wasted his breath. The situation got no better. It got worse. When the clock showed two minutes left to play, Rockwell motioned to Stewart and sent him hurrying to the locker room with orders to have the board set up so he could do some badly needed between-half chalk-talk. With a minute left to play, he cleared the bench so there'd be no delay in getting the locker room set up; he didn't want to waste a second of those precious between-half minutes. The bench was hardly cleared before the terrible half ended and the scoreboard showed Dulane 23, Valley Falls 13.

Surprisingly, as Rockwell hurried the Big Reds ahead of him and down the corridor to the home team locker room, there was little noise from the fans. Angry as he was, Rockwell caught the significance of the crowd's apathy.

There was a reason for the Valley Falls supporters' unusual behavior tonight, and Rockwell knew what it was as well as anyone else. The Big Reds weren't fighting or playing together, and they were going to get beaten! A team that didn't fight and play together couldn't win.

"Thirteen points!"

"Ten points behind!"

"And going nowhere fast!"

"Hilton's only scored three points!"

"What's wrong with him?"

Chip could have answered that question. A player can't score if he doesn't have the ball, and he hadn't gotten hold of the ball more than six or seven times during the whole half. Dulane's three-men-in-line principle was keeping Taps and him and every other Big Red away from the basket.

Rockwell's locker room procedure seldom varied. Chip and every other varsity man knew the procedure by heart. The first two minutes the team rested while Rockwell studied the shot chart stats and the scorebook.

Then for six straight minutes the team got it. During those six minutes the only voice heard in the dressing room was Rock's. He used the marker board and the strategy board, which was a replica of the basketball court. Five of the pieces Rockwell used for men were painted red, and five were painted black.

Then there were two minutes of squad discussion. During those two minutes a player could offer suggestions or ask questions. With the minute it took to get to the dressing room and the minute it took to get back to the court, that left three minutes for practice out on the court before the second half began.

But there was no second-half practice tonight. Rock scanned the notes and the scorebook and then went to work on the board.

Rockwell said nothing at all while he was drawing; but when he finished, he began to talk.

"The bare outline here on the left shows the way Dulane sets up their zone, assuming the ball is at the point indicated, circle A. Note the three men in line.

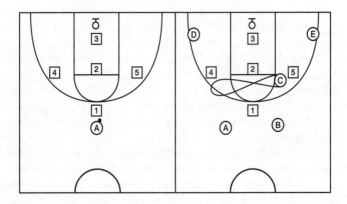

Players 1, 2, and 3. They try to keep in that formation, but shift with the ball.

"Now get this! This zone is set up so the shifts will keep three men between the ball and the basket at all times unless—unless—the ball is passed to a post or to a pivot player. Then they try to double up on him and tie up the ball.

"Now here on the right side of the board is the attack I want you to set up against it. It's a two-one-two formation. The setup isn't important! It's what you do with it that counts. When you've got it set up, I want you to start passing that ball around—or you're sure going to get beat!

"Morris, you and Rodriguez will be here in the backcourt, circles A and B. Schwartz, I want you to take Taps's place on the line, here where circle C is shown. And I want you to move as indicated by the flat figure 8 I've drawn there.

"Chip, you'll play in the left corner, circle D, and Taps, I want you in the right corner, circle E.

"Now we'll whip that ball around from one to another, and the first thing you know, someone will be open for a good shot! Everyone got it? OK! Now pay attention to these two plays. They'll work!"

Rockwell quickly flipped the board over to the clean side. Then he rapidly sketched in the plays.

"Now pay attention. You all know where you'll be playing. Watch! A passes to B who passes to C, that's Schwartz. Now, Red, you meet the pass and then dribble hard, as shown by the zigzag line. Dulane's 2, 3, and 5 will try to close in on you. Then you'll have the option of passing to D, that'll be Chip, or to E, Taps! Get it?

"Now on the right side of the board: A passes to B, and again the ball is passed to C, Schwartz. Red, this

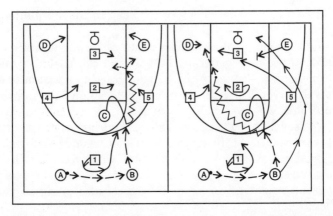

time you fake a dribble to your left, make it fast, and then dribble to the right, fast and hard. You'll find this time that Dulane's 2, 3, and 4 will try to close in on you, but you'll have a clear pass to Chip, D, and then, Chip, you should have a good, wide-open shot.

"But, Chip, if you can't get a shot, look at what Taps and B, that'll be either Morris or Rodriguez, have set up near the right side of the basket.

"Now Taps, you move to the side of the lane and stand there facing the basket. Watch Chip, though—he might pass you the ball. Stand there facing the basket, and then I want B, we'll say it's you, Speed, I want you to cut right behind Taps for a pass. Get it? Good! Remember, these plays work to the left just as well, and there's no change in anyone's play except Red's and the passer's. OK?

"Now, one thing more! The best way to beat any kind of zone—I said the *best* way—is to beat them down to your basket before they set up! Any questions? No? Well then, for Pete's sake, let's get out there and play ball! Come *on,* let's go!"

SICK AT HEART

The Big Reds tried, all right. But they didn't have it and couldn't get it. They'd lost the touch. Their shots didn't hit, and Dulane, conscious of the tremendous upset they were engineering, played perfect ball. On the offense, they monotonously passed, and passed, and passed as the minutes wore down, holding on to the ball and trying for a score only when they had a wide-open shot from close range. On the defense, all five wheeled back under the board and fought like tigers for the ball.

Then the Big Reds panicked, watching the clock and the scoreboard between passes and shots and defensive play. Just as Joe Kennedy had said in last Sunday's paper, the Big Reds came apart at the seams.

The Big Reds' fans couldn't believe it as they reluctantly filed out of the darkened gym. They kept looking at the scoreboard, still doubting their own eyes, trying to convince themselves the score was wrong. But it wasn't: Dulane 37, Valley Falls 30.

In the locker room, last year's state champions, confused and sick at heart, sat for a long time in front of their lockers.

Chip sat in that quiet locker room, hearing nothing except the running water splashing thinly in the shower, and he thought about many things. As he sat there he squirmed and turned and shifted his feet, feeling the strength well up in his body and hold there because there wasn't anything he could do about it. It required almost a physical effort to keep from leaping up and dashing back out on that gym floor to save a game that was already lost. He looked at Speed and Red and Taps and could tell they felt the same way.

But he didn't look at Mike because something he'd said in one of the huddles had hurt Chip most of all.

"You mean just because we don't give you the ball so you can take all the shots and make all the points!"

Chip Hilton didn't look up anymore that night or the next day at the Sugar Bowl. On Sunday, he never once looked at the papers but studied most of the day in his room. His heart was heavy and sore. Sunday evening, when his mom and Baxter were watching TV, Chip went down to the lab because it was the quietest place in the house. He needed to be alone so he could think.

There he found water dripping from the tap in the sink and some cigarette ashes beside the filing cabinet. He noticed those things, but his mind was too troubled to pay much attention. Nothing mattered right then except the barrier between the guys, which was building higher each day.

CHAPTER 11

Not JUs but Big Reds

HENRY ROCKWELL had spent a gloomy weekend, and nothing had happened today to lift his spirits. He swung around in his big leather chair, which had accompanied him from his dingy office in the old Central School to his book-and picture-lined private office in this modern high school building, and gazed out the window, across the lawns and beyond Ohlsen Stadium.

Rockwell wasn't worried because his team had lost a game. Long ago he'd learned "you can't win 'em all!" But the veteran mentor was deeply concerned about the Big Reds' steady decline in team play and spirit. It was an athletic disease that, similar to cancer, was hard to define and difficult to cure.

This team was plummeting down a steep canyon, and he knew he had to do something about it—quickly. The success of the entire season hinged on the next four or five games, maybe the next two. If this team went into a real tailspin, he'd have to be prepared to do something drastic. But what?

Rockwell sat for a long time, staring at the blue sky that stretched endlessly across the valley, and then he turned abruptly back to his desk and picked up another anonymous letter that had arrived in the day's mail. Muttering something uncomplimentary about the cowardly writer and crumpling up the sheet of paper, he made a neat two-pointer in the wastebasket in the corner.

But something in that anonymous letter had aroused Rockwell's appreciation for a good fight in a worthy cause. A few minutes later, Chet Stewart and the JVs were surprised to receive their second visit from Coach Rockwell in less than a week. Rockwell rarely trespassed upon his assistant's practice periods and seldom called upon the Little Reds for a scrimmage against the varsity because it was no contest and of little benefit to either team.

Today, Rockwell smiled at the group standing quietly waiting for him to speak.

"You men feel real tough this afternoon?"

They nodded eagerly and Captain Teddy Rice voiced their feelings. "Yes, sir. Almost tough enough to knock off the varsity!"

Rockwell nodded his head approvingly. "That's what I wanted to hear," he declared abruptly. "Coach, bring 'em over to the gym at 4:30!"

Pop Brown, Valley Falls's veteran trainer, was about the only cheerful person in the Big Reds' dressing room that afternoon. He tried to raise the spirits of the players who were dressing so slowly and quietly.

"Look here, now," he said, stopping directly in front of Chip. "Just because you all had a bad night against Dulane ain't no reason for us to forget there's other games comin'! One game ain't gonna stop us!"

NOT JUS BUT BIG REDS

Chip smiled weakly. "You're right, Pop," he affirmed, squaring his jaw. "That'll be the last one we lose!"

Soapy Smith had been unusually quiet, and when Soapy was quiet in a locker room—or anywhere else—things were bad. Now he tried to help Pop cheer up his teammates. "Aw, come on you guys," he pleaded. "Let's snap out of it! We've got that one out of our system. Now we can really rip the cords!"

Soapy's words had no effect. The Big Reds were down. Way down.

A little later, right after the warm-up drill, the JVs hustled out on the south end of the court.

Soapy Smith got a kick out of that. "Look," he growled, "*just* what I need—fresh meat!"

It was fresh meat, all right. The JVs were up, and the varsity took it too easy. The Little Reds fought the "big team" to a standstill. Stewart had matched Brevin against Chip, and, much as Chip wanted to help Brevin, he didn't take it easy. He gave Brevin a tough time. But then Chip Hilton could give any player in the state a tough time.

When Rockwell's whistle ended the scrimmage, everyone on the varsity was surprised to see him stop the JVs and ask Teddy Rice, Scottie Peck, and Brevin Barnes to remain behind.

"Now what's he up to?" Soapy growled.

They found out the next night, for those three guys were the first players out on the floor for *varsity* practice. They were embarrassed and a bit scared, but they were proud to be there—on the varsity!

The Valley Falls state champions knew Rock and his bluffs. They joked about this musty coaching strategy designed to scare them into his way of thinking.

"The old goat thinks we're going to fall for that?" Soapy chuckled.

All that week the Big Reds exchanged winks and sly smiles as Rockwell tried first Teddy Rice, and then Scottie Peck, and finally Brevin Barnes in varsity positions. In spite of their knowledge of Rock's methods, the Big Reds poured it on each newcomer. Rockwell enjoyed the practices, too, because the varsity was doing exactly what he wanted them to do. He wanted to see if they could take it.

The kids showed they could take it, all right, and they could give it too! Teddy Rice, captain of the JV team, was five feet eight inches and 150 pounds of fighting fury. Anyone watching Teddy play for five minutes could tell why the blue-eyed kid with the short blond hair had been elected captain of the Little Reds; he didn't know when or how to quit.

Scottie Peck was five feet ten inches and weighed around 160. He moved a lot like Speed Morris—maybe not quite so fast, but with the same drive. Scottie was a fine dribbler, a good rebounder, and showed signs of being a good backcourt leader.

Brevin Barnes was six feet one inch, but there all comparison with his JV teammates ended. Brevin was extremely slender; but his muscles were long, and he was wiry and moved with deceptive speed. One look at his long arms, big hands, and the ease with which he handled a basketball told the story on Brevin. He was a natural.

So the three JV kids took all the Big Reds could give and came back for more. As each one played, the other two sat on the bench and rooted for him. Before the week was over, the kids were no longer JVs but Big Reds, and the older guys, with the exception of Mike Rodriguez, moved over and made room for them on the varsity squad.

Mike Rodriguez carried the hazing a bit too far with Brevin Barnes, but Brevin never indicated he was aware of Mike's persecution. He just kept playing and looking better and better until the respect in Speed's, Red's, Soapy's, and Taps's eyes increased every day.

Chip got a surprise Wednesday. Pop told him not to dress when he arrived for practice. "The Rock wants to see you in his office, Chipper."

Chip paused outside Rockwell's office. Now what?

Chip had been in that office many times during the past three years, and he knew a lot about it. Yet, each time he visited, he was still thrilled by the pictures that hung on the walls and by the rows of sports and record books filling the bookcases.

When Chip knocked and entered, Rockwell jumped up and grabbed his hat and coat. "You ready?" he asked, smiling.

Chip was confused. "I—"

"Don't worry about it! We're going for a drive this afternoon, you and I. No practice for us. We're going over to Delford on a little scouting expedition. You know what's going on over there, don't you?"

Chip knew all right. Delford was tangling with Southern, and he'd sure like to see that game. The problem was he had to work.

Rockwell knew what Chip was thinking. "No work for you tonight either. I called your boss and he said it'd be all right as long as 'we win Friday night at Southern.'"

Chip enjoyed the drive to Delford. Rockwell didn't talk too much, and, when he did, it wasn't about basketball. Rockwell knew boys, and he knew his team's captain was just as concerned about the team as he was.

Anytime Delford played it was a hot evening. What the team might lack in ability it made up in fight, and tonight was a red-letter evening. Southern was leading Section Two, and Delford had its best team in years.

Southern was a junior team. The previous year Russell Whitcomb had decided to rebuild his team and had placed five sophomores on the starting five. The kids had started slowly and then had caught fire and burned up the league. In fact, the kids had just missed a bid to the state championships.

Back intact this year, they'd won eight in a row and were looking better every game. Still, winning at Delford was a tough assignment no matter how good the team. When the teams lined up for the tipoff, it was easy to see the Southerners lacked the height and weight to compete with Delford's Red Henry and his tall team-mates. The only exception was Southern's captain, a stocky six-footer with a square jaw and big, sloping shoulders.

"Hey, Whitcomb, that your JV team?"

"Where'd you get those scarecrows?"

"Past those kids' bedtime. Take 'em home!"

"We'll chase 'em home!"

But Delford didn't chase those kids home. They were fast and clever, and they were fighters. The best fighter on the floor was the Southern captain, Bill Berrien, a fighting rebel who dominated the defensive backboard as though he owned it. Slowly, the Southern kids crawled out in front and stayed there. In the third quarter, Southern's slender center fouled out, and the Delford supporters took hope. Red Henry was six-six, and Berrien, who switched over to the center spot, was only a little guy—or so it seemed.

"Now you got 'em, Red!"

"Get the ball to Red!"

But Bill Berrien was fast and strong, and he liked it rough. When Red Henry tried to push him around, the Southern captain really went to work.

NOT JUS BUT BIG REDS

Chip was busy making notes on the individual Southern players, and Rockwell was concentrating on their offense and defense. Chip couldn't help marveling at the fight and hustle of the Southern captain. He was faking and feinting and dribbling around Henry as though he were standing still on the offense. On defense, Berrien played in front of Henry, on the sides, and seemed to know just where Henry was weakest.

With two minutes to go, Southern led by three points, and the game degenerated into a dogfight. But the Southern kids fought like champions and won the grudging admiration of the home crowd by lasting it out to win 46-41.

While Chip and Coach Rockwell were scouting Southern at Delford, Valley Falls town fans were getting another dose of run-and-gun basketball. Tonight the opposition was the Clinton Big Five, and the game was being played at the Y.

John Schroeder, Doc Jones, little Paddy Jackson, and about every other hoop fan in town was there, not to mention the Big Red varsity and the JVs. It was a good show, all right—all the more so, perhaps, because the floor was small and, under T. A. K. Baxter's system, a player could shoot from nearly any spot on the floor. That's exactly what the Independents did! It seemed they fired it up as soon as they got the ball across midcourt and then banged in after the rebound, running the visitors dizzy. It was no contest.

The Clinton Big Five, comprised of former high school and a few college players who'd slowed down, didn't have a chance to cope with Baxter's slam-bang, racehorse style of play.

Speed Morris, Mike Rodriguez, Soapy Smith, and Red Schwartz were sitting together in the last row of seats high up by the windows, and what they saw didn't improve their attitudes. They looked down at Baxter, now substituting freely since his team was out in front by thirty points. Although no one would put the wish into words, each of the high school players wondered what it would be like if Baxter were coaching them. It would really be something to score twenty or thirty points a game!

Baxter was riding the crest of a wave. The sports news he was giving to Pete Williams and Joe Kennedy had drawn them into his corner. They wanted to give the colorful stranger all the publicity they could. He was news. They didn't overlook his pottery background, either, because local readers ate up anything and everything printed about both basketball and pottery.

Baxter was just about ready to spring his carefully baited trap on J. P. Ohlsen. He had the formulas all set, but he still needed those five pieces of pottery down in the Hilton basement. They represented the kind of ware he wanted Ohlsen to think he'd produced with domestic clay and his secret formulas—"T. A. K."

But there was still a flaw in his plan. He knew the Hilton kid spent a few minutes in the lab almost every day, and Chip would surely miss the five pieces of ware that always sat in plain view on the workbench.

Working carefully, Baxter had made a rough copy of one of the pieces and fearfully substituted it for one of Chip's priceless pieces. He'd placed it behind the others, hoping Chip wouldn't examine it too carefully.

Now, as Baxter sat on the Independents' bench, he kept looking at his watch. Before he caught his 11:30 flight, he wanted to be sure he'd have time to run out to the Hiltons' and pick up the bag in which he'd carefully packed the priceless piece. He knew a place where he could have five reasonable duplicates made. Once he had the five duplicates, he could put those on Chip's shelf and take Bill Hilton's beautiful originals to his appointment with J. P. Ohlsen.

On the way home, Chip and Rockwell talked over the game and the fine team they were to meet at Southern Friday night.

"They're good, Chip," Rockwell commented. "*Very* good! We'll have to be better than we've been for a long time if we're going to take 'em."

Nothing more was said then for a long stretch of snow-lined road. The two friends, just about as close as coach and player can get, sat there wondering and worrying about the Big Reds and what had happened to them. Later, Chip's thoughts swung around to Baxter's brand of basketball that had caught on in Valley Falls. He cautiously asked Rockwell if he'd known of Baxter when he was at State.

"No, Chip," Rockwell said thoughtfully, "I don't ever remember hearing about him. Why?"

"Oh, I don't know, Coach, except I couldn't find anything about him in Dad's old scrapbooks, and I was just wondering—"

Rockwell had never met Baxter, but he hadn't missed any of the articles about the Independents and their style of play. He certainly hadn't failed to get the significance of the little digs Kennedy and Williams had been taking at him in the papers.

Furthermore, he knew Baxter was supposed to have known Chip's father and that the man had moved into the Hilton home. He knew Chip Hilton well enough to know that the teenager was particularly worried about that.

"I understand he was supposed to have played there, Chip," Rockwell said slowly. "Would you like me to find out more about him?"

Chip didn't answer that question right away. He wanted to think it over. It seemed to him a little like spying on someone. Then he thought of his mother and suddenly decided to let Rockwell help him clear up his doubts.

"Coach," he said hesitantly, "could you find out if Mr. Baxter really went to State? I mean about the time my father did?"

"Why, sure, Chip. That's easy. I'll call tomorrow."

When Rockwell dropped Chip off at home, it was midnight, but Mary Hilton was waiting up for him.

"Did you have a good time, Chip?"

"I sure did, Mom. Southern won and that's bad news for us Friday night. How did the Independents make out?"

"Oh, they won by a big score, 103 to something. Mr. Baxter was telling me about it before he left."

"Left?"

"Yes, he said he had a meeting with his publisher in Chicago."

"He coming back?"

"Sure. He said he wouldn't be finished here for another two or three weeks. There was a big article about him in the paper tonight—on the front page. He's leaving for England around the first of February. Where did I put that paper? Here it is."

About that time, T. A. K. Baxter, self-styled author and leading authority on American pottery, was sitting in economy, flying to Chicago. As he sat looking out the window at the shadowy landscape, his mind was deeply concerned with his plan. This trip was going to cut heavily into the balance of his funds. Still, the thing had to go through now, or he'd be in a real mess.

He thought of that one piece of ware he'd worked so laboriously to make, and, for a moment, he worried about what would happen if the kid examined it closely. But it was too late now to do anything but hope for the best. With good luck he'd be back in Valley Falls by the first of the week with the five substitute pieces of pottery he needed to make his plan foolproof. The duplicates wouldn't have to be perfect, but they'd have to be passable.

No matter what Baxter told himself, his mind wouldn't rest. Bill Hilton's son had probably handled those five pieces of ware a hundred times, and he was no chump when it came to pottery—even if he was only a kid.

CHAPTER 12

Just Beneath the Surface

SOUTHERN, LOCATED in the extreme southern part of Section Two, straddled the river separating the two states. The first settlers and the store at the fording point on the river, and eventually the post office which was housed in the store, had remained on the north side of the river and that was why the town of Southern was in the state and in Section Two. It was a sleepy town most of the time. In the summer it got extremely hot in the afternoons, reason enough for a slower pace. In the winters, the decreased river traffic was a good excuse to hibernate.

But Southern wasn't sleepy this winter, and the reason was Southern's high school varsity basketball team. The five kids comprising the starting team had played together through middle school, in the first year of high school, and then, last year, had played intact as Southern's varsity. They'd played like champions too. After a shaky start, they'd become strong in the last half of the season, losing to the Big Reds at Valley Falls but beating Steeltown a week later to put the Iron Men out of the running for Section Two honors. Thus, Valley Falls moved into the runner-up position behind Weston. That had given Valley Falls a chance to play in the All-State tournament at University, and the Big Reds had come through to win the state championship.

The Big Reds left Valley Falls Friday afternoon at 2:00, and the three-hour bus trip brought them to the Southern Hotel at exactly 5:00, just as Rogers had informed the hotel manager when he'd made the reservations. They'd stopped on the way for a brief meal as they usually did, and after their two-hour rest, would be ready for the game. After the game, they'd have their team meal before returning to the hotel for the night.

Rockwell, last off the bus, stopped to chat with the driver and was surprised when he entered the lobby to see his players still standing around waiting. Rogers and Stewart were engaged in earnest conversation with the desk clerk. Biggie Cohen was standing nearby with a list of room pairings. Rock approached the desk and asked Rogers, "What's the trouble, Prof? Didn't they get our reservations?"

"Yes, Hank. But the manager wants to see us in his office."

Rockwell looked keenly at Rogers and then at the clerk before following Rogers to the manager's office.

"What is it, Prof?"

Rogers shook his head. "Something's not right."

The new manager of the Southern Hotel had been in the hotel business for many years, and he knew how to handle people. His keen eyes quickly evaluated the two educators. He extended his hand and greeted them like long-lost brothers, his smile as broad as the Mississippi River.

"Gentlemen, my name is Bo Hankins. Glad to meet you, Rogers, and you, Coach Rockwell. Sit down, gentlemen. Hope you had a nice trip down. Well, you fellows had better be good. These kids of ours are red-hot!"

Prof Rogers cleared his throat and managed to interpose, "We're hav—"

Hankins nodded his head and kept right on going. "Now, er, Mr. Rogers, I'm in sort of a predicament. Unfortunately, we overbooked our rooms, and we're jammed up here. Now, don't worry, we got your reservations, all right, and we'll be able to take care of most of your group, all right, but we'd like to send a few of you over to a little place we have for just such emergencies. I'm sure you can understand how it is in the hotel business."

Hankins looked at them expectantly, but when there was no response, he continued amiably, "Now there's a nice place practically right around the corner. In fact, we've already called and made arrangements for Mr. Barnes and Mr. Brown." He turned to a young man sitting at a small desk.

"Bill, why don't you go down to the desk and get the rest of the rooms assigned. Have Catlin take our two Valley Falls guests over to Byrds."

Rockwell leaned forward in his chair and looked the manager straight in the eyes. Then he spoke softly but with a bit of a rasp in his voice, "Are you trying to tell us, Mr. Hankins, that specific people on our team will have to go somewhere else?"

Hankins nodded his head and smiled. "That's it, Coach. We had some trouble last year when one of the big city teams came down, so we've come up with this arrangement. I'm glad you understand."

Rockwell stood up slowly and shook his head. "I think I understand more than I want to," he said firmly.

"We have nineteen players plus our coaching staff, and we always travel together. We never break up our group." He turned to Rogers.

"Didn't you tell Mr. Hankins how many of us to expect?"

"I sure did, Rock, and he confirmed our reservations!"

Hankins was on his feet now, aware for the first time that these men might not be as easily handled as he'd wished. "Now, er, look here, Coach. We got the fax, all right. But—"

Rockwell dismissed the voluble manager with a wave of his hand. "Mr. Hankins," he said coolly, "this is both immoral and illegal, and you know it! We're insulted and chagrined with your bigotry! Maybe a few reporters would like to interview us in front of your hotel before our bus leaves for Valley Falls—before the game."

"Oh now, Coach, that's not the attitude to take. We're proud to have you high school groups stopping here at Southern, and we don't want to disappoint you in any way. I tell you what—I'll call Coach Whitcomb at the high school." A worried Bo Hankins withered behind his desk.

While Hankins's secretary was calling the high school, the hotel manager was trying to convince Rockwell he hadn't meant any harm, saying he sure hoped he hadn't given Valley Falls the wrong impression, that the hotel business sure was a trying field. Finally, he got Russell Whitcomb, Southern's coach, on the phone, and Whitcomb said he'd be right down.

Rockwell waited in the office, scarcely hearing or believing Hankins, while Rogers went downstairs to join Chet Stewart and the team.

Coach Henry Rockwell was a perfectionist in his coaching, and every detail that concerned his basketball team was important. His coaching went beyond the basketball court, which was one of the big reasons for his success through the years. The veteran coach expected his athletes to conduct themselves like gentlemen in their off-court behavior, at home or on the road.

Valley Falls athletes learned early in their athletic careers to take pride in themselves and their personal appearance. The group of teenagers lounging in the lobby would have been a credit to any school. Yet, as they stood in little groups, talking and laughing, their nervousness was easily detected. They knew this delay in Rockwell's regular trip routine was unusual.

Each player tried to act as if it were normal to hang around a hotel lobby before checking in. Biggie Cohen went from one player to the next ostensibly making up the room pairings he already knew by heart, and Chet Stewart corralled the JVs and began quizzing them on some of his basketball principles.

Pop Brown and Brevin Barnes were busily studying a large painting that hung over the lobby fireplace but which neither really saw.

When Rogers came down from the office and suggested they take a ten or fifteen minute walk "to loosen up their legs after the long ride," everyone was relieved. But this, too, was a departure from the regular procedure, and much as they tried to be their usual selves, it was impossible. They straggled slowly along the sidewalk, and when they neared the hotel coming back, everyone unconsciously slowed down, reluctantly entering the lobby.

Not long after Rogers left Hankins's office, Coach Whitcomb came hurrying in, obviously disturbed. He'd gleaned only an inkling of the difficulty over the phone, but he knew exactly what Rockwell was up against. One glance at the Valley Falls coach's tense face was enough to tell him the problem Hankins had on his hands.

Russ Whitcomb was a good-looking, friendly man in his late thirties. Now in his third year as head coach at Southern, he'd been remarkably successful in football as well as basketball. He was extremely concerned now because he admired Rockwell very much, and he valued his friendship. The warmth of his greeting to Rockwell didn't escape Hankins; and while the two coaches conversed in low tones, the worried manager considered his problem from all angles.

Hankins was thinking maybe he could weasel out of this some way. The Valley Falls group would be here only one night, and they were leaving early in the morning. He'd already set up a special dining room for them. Maybe the smartest thing would be to give them their rooms.

Whitcomb and Rockwell were both relieved when Hankins abruptly announced, "I think I can work around this situation. I'll have the front desk give Coach Rockwell's group all their rooms. I'll rearrange any other guests as needed, Russ, this time. Coach Rockwell, you come with me and I'll get you a good room, myself."

There was little respect in Rockwell's eyes or in his heart for this man. "That won't be necessary. I'll take any room."

Rockwell, unpacking his suitcase, seemed to take it for granted that everything was fine now that the hotel situation was ironed out. But Whitcomb, sitting in a chair by the window trying to figure out a way to approach the Valley Falls coach, feared it wasn't.

"Rock," he finally plunged, "I don't know what to say. I know it's ludicrous. The people down here are good. I just can't understand why a few people seem so bent on carrying on as they do. I guess those feelings have come down through the years and the generations. Unfortunately, it has been passed down to a handful of kids too. The great majority of our kids hang out and do things together and are friends, but a few of the adults—if you can call 'em that—just won't wise up! I don't know how your team might be treated by those few idiotic fans."

Rockwell listened quietly. He knew Russ Whitcomb was a good man—sincere, thoughtful, courteous, and fair in his thinking. As Rockwell looked at the young coach, his mouth slanted in that friendly, crooked smile of his. "Russ," he said softly, "I understand. But there's another side to this issue. We at Valley Falls believe all students are entitled to all the privileges and honors the school offers. More than that, Pop Brown is a member of our staff. Brevin Barnes is one of our students and has shown he's a good enough basketball player to earn a place on our squad, maybe on our first team, and, well, if any member of our group is excluded or slighted, then we would all have to go."

"Rock," Whitcomb assured, "you and I feel the same way. Still, I want to give you a sense of what this place can be like. One time I arranged a home scrimmage with a predominately black high school, and a few people in town raised such a fuss when they heard about it that I thought for sure I was going to be fired. One school board member even made a point—off the record, of course—of telling me specifically that the next time I pulled a stunt like that my teaching job here in Southern might be gone. They follow the rules on the surface, but it's just beneath the surface where we have to watch out.

"Also, I didn't notice Speed Morris in the lobby when I came in, so I thought maybe Valley Falls was going to

JUST BENEATH THE SURFACE

do what Steeltown did with Minor when they played us here. We played football and basketball at their place, but they didn't bring him along when they came here so the few loud mouths in the crowd wouldn't get on him."

Rockwell shook his head. "I've never heard of anything like that, but I wouldn't cheapen my school, my team, or myself by being a party to any such thing you mentioned with Minor. I don't believe any real educator would either. No, sir! But just so you know, Speed's home with the measles. Otherwise, he'd be here too! Bet Hankins would *really* like that!" he commented dryly.

"Tell you what, Rock," Whitcomb said, "suppose I call Murtagh. He's the principal. Great guy! We'll go over to his office."

Half an hour later, after making sure the players and coaching staff were all settled in their assigned rooms, Rockwell met the principal of Southern's high school, T. R. Murtagh. The principal listened soberly as Whitcomb told him about the incident with Bo Hankins and how Rockwell felt.

"Rock and I are wondering about the crowd tonight, T. R., and, well—" Whitcomb looked at Murtagh hopefully and continued, "well, that's why we're here."

As Russ Whitcomb talked, Murtagh's expression grew more serious. When he finally spoke, his voice expressed deep concern.

"Russ is right, Coach. The situation is a serious one."

Murtagh paused, and the silence was deep and heavy. Then in a thoughtful voice the principal continued: "Personally, I don't know of any better time than tonight to see just how deep the prejudice lies in this town. The citizens of Southern are keenly interested in this fine basketball team of ours.

"Certainly, if fellowship is to be found anywhere, it should be found in the hearts of those who believe in sportsmanship and the important value of sports as an educational force in our schools.

"We must keep in mind that this requires a change of attitudes for a few members in this community. That's a pretty serious objective. We may be treading on quicksand. However, I'm willing to do my part, and, if you're willing to go along, Russ—well, then, let's do the right thing. Personally, I won't mind doing a little job-searching if we can cause a few people with prejudice-filled hearts to do a little soul-searching."

All this time the Valley Falls coach hadn't said a word. He'd been watching and listening to the two Southern educators, and his face clearly registered his admiration. Without a word, Rockwell got to his feet and shook hands with Principal Murtagh. However the game came out tonight—win, lose, or draw—here were two men he could respect.

CHAPTER 13

Southern Exposure

T. R. MURTAGH knew what he was talking about, all right. The citizens of Southern were very much aware of the championship potential of their kids—their kids who'd narrowly missed the state tournament last year and who were storming Section Two this year.

"Yep, the kids have won nine in a row!"

"Valley Falls knocked us out of the race last year!"

"Yeah, we'll pay 'em back for that tonight!"

"Rockwell better not use a zone tonight!"

"He's foxy, that old guy!"

"Lucky, you mean!"

"Best coach in the state!"

"Could be, but we've got the best team in the state!"

With the Southern JVs trimming the Little Reds by a score of 38-22, the Southerners expressed their joy in a thunderous cheer that could be heard blocks away. Of course, they didn't know that Scottie Peck, Teddy Rice, and Brevin Barnes had been moved up to the varsity and that without their help, the Valley Falls JVs were handicapped.

The veteran Big Reds knew it however. In some of their hearts, a smoldering resentment burned against the three boys who'd run out on their teammates just to sit on the varsity bench. When the team trotted out on the floor for the warm-up, those same veterans were a little bitter toward Rock, Chet, and even Pop, who'd made such a fuss over the new additions to the varsity squad.

The Southern fans greeted the Big Reds with a burst of applause. This fan-jammed gymnasium was a tribute to the reigning state champs. This was the game everybody in Southern had been waiting for.

The Big Reds went right into their three-lane warm-up drill. As the players cut under the basket for the pass, the shot, the rebound, and the hard, fast pass back to the center, scattered, ugly remarks punctuated the applause. Whispers began spreading throughout the gym.

On the bench, Henry Rockwell's ears burned. His heart fluttered and pressed high up in his chest until there was a growing pain right under the knot in his tie and he had a tough time breathing. His mind was in turmoil, and he half wished he'd taken his team back to Valley Falls that afternoon.

Then Rockwell began to worry about the kids he'd brought down here, and the pain in his chest was replaced by a burning anger.

Just then, fortunately, the Southerners dashed out on the floor, and their fans got up on their feet and lifted the roof. These were their kids! The next state champions! These kids were putting Southern on the map!

The Southern band and cheering squad went into action, and most of the people there put thoughts of the black player on the Valley Falls squad out of their minds as they cheered their kids to the skies.

A few spectators continued to murmur and hiss. They wondered whether he was a regular on the Valley Falls team and what would happen if "that Rockwell" put him in against their kids. A few so-called "sportsmen" sitting in the bleachers near the floor at the end of the court where the Big Reds were warming up made some remarks that no true sportsman would ever make.

Brevin Barnes heard some of these remarks as he tried to concentrate on the warm-up drill, but he was new to the squad and had a lot of things on his mind. He got butterfingered and missed a couple of passes; then he missed the basket, and the laughter and the booing that followed the missed shot made things worse.

The Big Reds heard the jeers and the things being said, and they began to get mad. Chip Hilton slapped Brevin on the back and said, "Come on! Snap out of it!"

It was a good thing that right then Rockwell signaled them, and they all left the floor for the locker room. Southern went down to their locker room at the same time. In the interim, the Southern cheering squad and pep band went to work, and the crowd didn't have much chance to do anything but cheer.

A minute later, the two teams rushed out on the floor, and the cheering broke loose again. Those more concerned with Brevin Barnes than with the game were drowned out by the thundering roar. The fans who had directed the cutting remarks toward Brevin were temporarily stilled because he was sitting on the bench when the starting five walked onto the floor.

Captain Chip Hilton and Red Schwartz were at the forwards; Taps Browning, at center; and Mike Rodriguez and Soapy Smith, replacing Speed, were at the guards.

The Southern line-up was the same one that had breezed through nine straight games. Captain Bill Berrien was shaking hands with Chip Hilton; Bob Ford was smiling at Taps Browning, the top of Taps's head just one inch above Ford's. Little Buddy Glasco was gripping hands with Mike Rodriguez, and Rob Kimmel had grabbed Soapy Smith by the arm and they were slapping each other on the back. Gil Lydon and Red Schwartz, evenly matched, were pulling at each other's hands just as they had a year ago, and both were thinking the same thing, "I *would* draw you!"

Ford outjumped Taps, and it was Southern's ball. Chip immediately switched over and picked up Kimmel, Soapy took Gil Lydon, and Red checked Bill Berrien. Chip knew he would have his hands full with Kimmel. Rob Kimmel could hit from outside and was expert at driving around a defender if he was played tight.

Chip played him as close as he dared, but Kimmel got a three-pointer away; it never touched the rim as it swished through for the first score of the game. The crowd ate that up. Kimmel had put that Hilton kid in his place.

"Hey, Hilton! Having trouble?"

Chip heard some of those jibes as he broke downcourt. Bill Berrien dropped over in front of Chip, pointing and yelling, "I've got Hilton! Take Schwartz, Kim!"

Chip spurted and beat Berrien in to the basket, but it was wasted effort. When he pivoted and looked for the ball, he was just in time to see Mike Rodriguez dribble to the right-hand corner and let a wild three-point attempt fly at the basket.

Right then, Chip's respect for Bill Berrien went up 50 percent. Berrien faced the basket and blocked him expertly away from the rebound. When Chip sidestepped to the left, Berrien shifted swiftly and surely, again placing himself between Chip and the board. Then he leaped high in the air with perfect timing, pulled in the ball with one hand, and threw it hard and true down the left sideline to the five-foot-two-inch Glasco.

Glasco was off like a shot, dribbling around and past Rodriguez as if Mike were nailed to the floor. Soapy, dropping back with his eyes glued on Lydon, took after Glasco a second too late, catching the little dribbler just short of the basket. Soapy couldn't stop the shot, and Southern was out in front, 5-0, in less than a minute of play.

Soapy grabbed the ball just as it dropped through the net, stepped out of bounds, and fired a hard baseball pass right back upcourt to Rodriguez. Mike then pivoted around with the ball, dribbled into the corner and let fly with another errant shot.

Chip followed-in, but Bill Berrien was right there between him and the basket again, boxing him out and grabbing the rebound. And that's the way it went—Berrien controlling the Big Reds' rebounds and starting the Southern break rolling each time with a perfect catcher's peg far down the court. At the end of the quarter, Southern was out in front, 14-8. Soapy had hit with a jumper from the free-throw line, and Chip had dropped in a free throw when Berrien had body-blocked him away from the basket.

The crowd liked what they saw. Berrien was tying Chip in a knot, forcing him away from the basket time after time. Throughout the half the Big Reds showed almost no offense. It was "up the floor and let it fly." At the half, the score was Southern 29, Valley Falls 19.

Rockwell's locker room talk was fiery and bitter, sending the Big Reds out on the court fighting mad. But it didn't mean a thing. Southern took up where they'd left off. At the end of the third quarter, they were out in front, 43-30.

Something happened at the start of the fourth period that foreshadowed the collapse of the Big Reds. Schwartz and Rodriguez nearly came to punches when Red called Mike a gunner. Rodriguez came right back and accused Schwartz of being a ball hog. Chip called time.

Rockwell took care of it by sending Bill English in for Schwartz and little Lefty Peters in for Rodriguez. The substitution seemed to give the Big Reds a shot in the arm. Chip got the ball for a change and canned six quick points, drawing resounding cheers from his teammates by getting away from Berrien three straight times. Then Southern called a time-out. With five minutes to go, the score was Southern 43, Valley Falls 36.

When play resumed, Glasco turned up the heat and scored twice, faking Peters out of position and dribbling in for easy layups. Chip again called time. The crowd's continuous roar clearly indicated their feelings of superiority; their kids were dominating this important game with the state champions. All the while the fans were riding the Big Reds and cheering their kids, Rockwell had been thinking about Brevin Barnes, mentally debating whether or not to send him into this game in this town.

Caution held him back for an instant. Then he remembered his words to Chet Stewart: "The best player gets the job." That did it! Rockwell knew that at any other time and at any other place he'd have substituted Barnes for Peters. He didn't hesitate another second. He turned and almost lifted Barnes to his feet.

"In for Peters, Brevin," he said sharply, "and take Glasco—"

Brevin Barnes's startled eyes were wide and unbelieving, but the paralyzing grip of steel fingers digging into his arm and the compelling fire in Rockwell's piercing black eyes shocked him into action. Three long strides carried him to the scorer's table where he reported for Peters. Then he was back in the huddle between Rockwell and Chip.

The tumult of exultation that had subsided during the time-out now arose again, only this time it was elevated by a swelling babble of jeering.

In front of the home bench, Coach Russ Whitcomb was talking earnestly to his players. One player shook his head and sat down on the bench, and another followed. A single cheer went up, evidently for those two who refused to play against the black athlete. But when Whitcomb, anticipating this reaction, motioned two other players, they eagerly rose from the bench and reported to the scorer.

When the Big Reds started out on the floor, the explosive response of the fans rocked the building. The bedlam of cheers, punctuated by yells and catcalls, was too much for a sensitive person like Brevin Barnes. He turned and walked back to the bench. Rockwell blocked him at the edge of the court, and Barnes stopped. His stricken eyes lifted to Rockwell's face. His voice trembled a little as he whispered to the coach. Soft as his words were, Rockwell heard them—louder than all the noise in the gym.

"I don't want to play against them if they don't want to play against me, Coach."

Barnes sank down onto the bench. His head dropped forward, and he never heard a thing.

It's the small moments that take our breath away. The shouting and the yelling died down a bit then. It almost ceased entirely a second later when the captain of Southern High School's basketball team walked deliberately over to the Valley Falls bench, reached down, and grasped Brevin Barnes by the hand. He led Brevin Barnes onto the floor where he played out the remainder of the game.

When the game was over, deafening cheers rose up from the packed stands. Brevin never knew that many of those cheers were for him.

When that great crowd of hoop-crazy fans filed soberly out of the building a few minutes later, they knew Southern had upset the state champions. They also knew that, for some reason, the victory hadn't been as thrilling as they'd expected. The score had been 50-47, but some knew Valley Falls had scored eleven points in the last few minutes while Southern scored only three. Some even grudgingly admitted Brevin Barnes was a good basketball player.

While some were bitter and some were angry, others were ashamed. A few were proud, like the middle-aged father and mother who strolled quietly toward their modest home down near the river, where the nameplate Berrien was stenciled on the mailbox. These two and many others could still see Southern's noble young captain leading the athlete from Valley Falls out onto the floor.

Most of those who walked out into the clean, cool night air after that great Southern victory somehow felt pride in the realization that the captain of the kids who represented their high school, as well as their town, was a courageous, bighearted teenage athlete who wasn't afraid to be a man.

CHAPTER 14

Defeat and Division

BO HANKINS, the effusive, efficient, and clever manager of Southern Hotel, was surprised when the Valley Falls High School basketball team checked out that same night. He was relieved, he had to admit to himself, but he professed to be extremely sorry when he said good-bye to Prof Rogers and Chet Stewart.

"Tell the coach not to forget us the next time he's in Southern. And better luck next time."

"Something tells me Coach Rockwell won't be forgetting about you for a long time!" Stewart shot back.

The Big Reds were glad to get out of that town and headed for home. They'd all expressed that desire when Rockwell said they could go to a movie if they wanted to after the game. But they didn't want to and they said so. They wanted to go home! Rockwell and Rogers agreed it was a good idea.

It was past 10:30 when their bus pulled away from the Hotel; with good luck they'd be home in two and a half hours. The driver clicked off the lights, and the only conversation was the muffled talk of some of the JVs who hadn't understood and hadn't caught the significance of the crowd's reaction to Brevin Barnes.

Most of the players slouched down in their seats and tried to sleep, but Chip Hilton, Brevin Barnes, Soapy Smith, and Biggie Cohen were wide awake. They were thinking about many things.

Chip was thinking about his mom and how she must have felt when she heard the score. Then he began thinking about the wide rift in the feelings and in the play of the Big Reds. Mike and Red and even Soapy had gone completely overboard with the kind of basketball the Independents were playing. Then Chip's thoughts swung around to the stranger, T. A. K. Baxter. Rockwell had called the university just as he said he would and they'd confirmed, "Yes, sure, Rock, we had a Baxter here. Played one year of varsity basketball, I think. But there was a Baxter here. . . ."

Brevin Barnes was still in a fog. The evening had been a nightmare. He was disconsolate that the team had lost, though he knew he'd given his level best.

Biggie Cohen was fed up with Mike Rodriguez and Red Schwartz. He also wondered about Speed's attitude. The team was being wrecked because of guys who'd been—and were still, he hoped—his friends. The team play was shot, and Chip wasn't getting the ball. Biggie didn't know what to do about it. He was most worried, though, about the tension between Chip, Speed, Red, and Mike. Biggie hoped Speed's being stuck home with the measles would straighten out his head.

Rockwell, in a front seat next to Rogers, hadn't spoken a word since he sat down. He was thinking back through the years to the time when he'd first realized the enormity of this racial question. There hadn't been enough progress. Still, he had to believe there were many more solidly grounded kids like Berrien, Barnes, and Hilton to set the right standard.

Late that night, snowflakes began to swirl. When Mary Hilton called Chip the next morning, the snow was ankle deep. Chip hustled outside and began shoveling a path to the sidewalk. He was glad to have something to do so he wouldn't have to talk about the game. But he couldn't entirely escape his mom's questions over their pancakes and juice. Mary Hilton sensed Chip's despondency, and she couldn't resist trying to help him.

"What's happening to the team, Chip?"

Chip took a sip of juice and then told his mom all about the incident at Southern and about the team and how it wasn't a team at all now. He was almost bitter as he talked, choosing his words carefully and trying to be fair. It was as though he was trying to figure it all out for himself as he spoke.

"Bill Berrien was great, Mom! That crowd was close to a mob, I guess. Berrien just clasped hold of Brevin's hand and led him out on the floor. Then he and the Southern guys lined up and we lined up and the game went on.

"And, Mom," Chip reflected, "Berrien played against Barnes. He'd been playing against me, you know, but he shifted over against Brevin for the rest of the game. When it was over, he shook hands with Brev, slapped him on the back, and walked clear over to our bench with him."

Mrs. Hilton knew that wasn't all that was worrying her son, so she waited patiently for him to continue.

"Mom," Chip began anxiously, "have you noticed any difference in Speed, Red, and Soapy lately? When the season first started, we worked hard as a team. Now, it seems it's each guy for himself."

Chip then told his mother about Mike Rodriguez, about the way he'd been playing and what he'd said about Chip's high scoring. He told her about the team's obsession for individual scoring, but he was careful to leave Baxter out of it.

"Mike said I was ticked because I wasn't making all the points. Now I wish I hadn't said anything to him. I'm sure not going to say anything to anyone else."

Mary Hilton couldn't think of how to help her son in his predicament, so she probably did the best thing possible. She smiled encouragingly and told him she trusted his heart. Chip kissed his mom lightly on the cheek and trudged down Main Street to the Sugar Bowl. He had the first hour of that day to himself, and he was glad—he was in no mood to explain to Petey or to John Schroeder what had happened.

Midway in the morning, Petey came barging into the storeroom with Soapy right behind him. "Hey, Chip," he said excitedly, "look at what Kennedy says in today's *Times*. Here, read it!"

Chip reluctantly read the column while Petey and Soapy hung over his shoulder.

Times and Sports
by Joe Kennedy

The Big Reds' hopes for the successful defense of their state title took another nose dive last night at Southern when the team from the big river section handed the locals their second straight setback by a score of 50-47.

The score is misleading. The game was anything but close. Valley Falls was completely subdued as early as the end of the first quarter when they trailed 14-8. During the second period, the Southerners took Valley Falls completely apart and led at the half, 29-19.

Things got worse in the third quarter, and at the end of the period, Southern led, 43-30. Coach Russ Whitcomb's team eased up in the fourth quarter, enabling the state champions to save a little face in what might easily have been a rout.

Brevin Barnes played in the final minutes of the game and looked just as good in a varsity uniform as he has looked with the Little Reds.

What's happened to Chip Hilton's shooting eye? Hilton's early season scoring spurt is holding his game average to 19.3 per game; but in the last four games, Hilton has scored 14, 12, 9, and 12 points, respectively. High-scoring records aren't broken with those totals.

Meanwhile, the Independents continued on their merry way to the establishment of all-time individual and team scoring records in our fair village, if not in the state.

And that brings to mind a thought for local civic and service clubs who've been groping around for a means of raising money for the Damon Runyon Cancer Fund: Why not stage a game at the high school between the Big Reds and the Independents? Local interest in the game would be tremendous!

Speculation and arguments—pro and con— abound about the Big Reds and their ability to cope with the hard-pressing, high-scoring attack used by Coach Baxter's hard-driving Independents.

Just for the record, let's check the Independents' scorebook: In seven games, they've scored exactly 648 points for an average of 92 points per game. Ninety-two points per game!

On the other side of the ledger, the Big Reds have scored 476 points in ten games for a game average of 47.6. What do you think of the idea, fans?

The Big Reds play Parkton at home next Friday night, January 17, and Weston away on Wednesday, the 22. The Independents play on the 15 and the 20. *Why not stage the Game on Saturday, January 25, for the Damon Runyon Cancer Fund?*

Soapy grabbed the paper, wadded it into a ball, and then threw it up at the ceiling. "Can you imagine that guy," he declared sarcastically. "Just because we lose a game. Hah! Besides, their games are longer than ours! Man, there's no comparison."

"What about the Independents, Chip?" Petey asked curiously. "You guys afraid of them? You think Rock would play them?"

Soapy turned as though he'd been stung by a hornet and nearly jabbed a finger through Petey's chest. "Afraid of them?" Soapy yelled incredulously. "Afraid of them?" he repeated. "Are you losin' your mind? Why, we'd kill 'em! Kill 'em, I tell you—kill 'em piece by piece!"

"Yeah?" Petey retorted, shaking a skinny forefinger in Soapy's face. "Yeah? You guys couldn't carry their shoes! You ain't got nobody on the whole team 'cept Chip, here, who can even hit the backboard! Who's gonna score for you? Huh? And who's gonna stop the break and shooting Baxter's taught 'em? Kill 'em! Hah! They'll beat you fifty points—easy! Looky here! Look at what Pete Williams says here in the *Post*! He says the same thing! Listen: 'Aside from the Cancer Fund benefits, the contest will give local hoop enthusiasts an opportunity to compare the run-and-shoot brand of basketball coached by T. A. K. Baxter with the more conservative style favored by

Rockwell. The Independents undoubtedly carry too many guns for the kids, but since the cause is worthwhile and the contest purely an exhibition, it seems a great idea. This reporter is all for it and all for the Cancer Fund!'"

Petey looked at Soapy triumphantly. "Well," he smiled smugly, "what do you think about that?"

Soapy was on the defensive now, but he wasn't at a loss for words. "Aw, what do those two bozos know about basketball!" he blurted aggressively. "Why, neither one of 'em ever played anything but horseshoes or lawn darts."

"And what's the matter with horseshoes?" he demanded. "Takes skill, don't it? Takes a good eye to make a ringer, don't it?"

Soapy was disgusted. "Skill? Good eye? Ringer? Hah! Let me out of here before I hang a ringer on your eye."

The argument between Petey and Soapy had company. It seemed everybody in town had gotten into it, and they all took sides.

Doc Jones thought the Independents were terrific: "They'll beat the kids by thirty points!"

John Schroeder stuck with Rockwell and with the Big Reds: "The kids play a sounder game. They have a better defense! The Independents have been playing pushovers!"

CHAPTER 15

A Revealing Wind

WHILE ROCKWELL was thinking about last year's state champions and what he could do to pull them together again, his players were thinking about the Independents and what they were going to do about them on Saturday, January 25. Reluctantly, the coach had yielded to public clamor and arranged the charity game with the Independents. Soapy, his old self again, led the verbal assault against the town team.

"Wait till we get at 'em. Wish we were playin' 'em this Saturday. We'll kill 'em!"

"Don't forget we've got two games before the twenty-fifth," Chip reminded him, "and they're both tough!"

"We'll start rolling now," Biggie stated confidently.

Speed Morris, well again but still somewhat weak, nodded his head grimly. "Maybe someone else can score for me," he said dryly. "If Chip doesn't outscore Joe Kelly, I'll stop playing basketball." He stopped abruptly and looked around at the circle of faces. Speed grinned as he continued, "The way I've been playing, it looks like I've stopped already."

If Rockwell had heard this conversation, he might have utilized a bit of psychology to bring his team together for the upcoming game with the Independents. But he wasn't there and perhaps didn't even realize what a deep impression the stranger had made on Mike, Speed, Red, and Soapy.

So all week he kept shifting his line-up and, as the novelty of the impending game with the Independents wore off, the players began to drift apart again.

When Chip got home after practice Thursday evening, he was feeling especially down. He opened the front door and met his mom in the center hall carrying the vacuum cleaner. "Hey, where you going with that?" he demanded, kissing her and gently taking it out of her hand.

Mary Hilton smiled. "I'm going upstairs to vacuum Mr. Baxter's room. He'll be home tomorrow. At least he said he'd be back on Friday."

Chip carried the vacuum upstairs and into the guest bedroom. The room had that stale tobacco odor that permeates a room when the windows have been tightly closed. Chip sniffed and, without thinking, opened the window. A gust of wind flooded the room and sent all the papers lying on the desk whirling around the room and onto the floor.

Chip hastily closed the window and helped his mom pick up the papers. They concerned formulas and pottery and were evidently being prepared for Mr. Baxter's book. Chip could tell that from the brief glance he gave them, but the thing that grabbed his and his mom's attention, causing them both to stare, was the newspaper picture of their houseguest. The photo headed a newspaper article that said it was one of a series that the distinguished chemist, T. A. K. Baxter, was writing about the history and development of ceramic engineering in American colleges and universities.

Chip and his mother scrutinized the clipping intently. "It doesn't even look like him," Chip said slowly.

Mrs. Hilton held the paper up to the light of the window and shook her head. "No, it doesn't," she agreed.

They both looked at the date. "But this picture was taken ten years ago, and Mr. Baxter didn't have a mustache then. The eyes seem the same, though, and he appears a lot heavier in the picture," Mrs. Hilton said.

Chip studied the eyes, but as far as he could see, there was no real resemblance. Nothing more was said, but that article had started Chip thinking again. Something about this man just didn't click. Chip wished he could put his finger on what it was.

All through dinner Chip couldn't get his mind off Baxter. He finished dinner and glanced at the clock. He had a few minutes left before it was time to leave for the Sugar Bowl so he decided to go down into the lab. Ever since reading the article and studying Baxter's picture, Chip had been thinking about pottery.

He unlocked the door, clicked on the light, and picked up one of the pieces of his father's pottery. The pieces of ware were of the same design and shape, and Chip ran his fingers lightly over each of the five. The last one was a little further back on the table, and as soon as Chip touched it, he noticed the difference. The finish was irregular, and the weight didn't seem the same. He wondered why he'd never noticed that before. But he replaced it and hurried off to the Sugar Bowl without thinking much more about it.

A REUEALING WIND

The flight into the airport arrived right on time at 2:27. T. A. K. Baxter and a handful of other passengers walked up the jet way as outbound passengers prepared to board.

Baxter was in excellent spirits and greeted two or three people he recognized on his way to his rental car. He held his carry-on with a tight grip. Locating his car, he carefully placed the bag on the seat beside him. He drove straight up Main Street, past the Sugar Bowl and up the little hill, and then to the right for three blocks till he reached the house at 131 Beech Street.

He'd have to proceed quickly with his plan now and start thinking about his approach to J. P. Ohlsen. As he placed the case gently on the front porch and fumbled in his pocket for the door key, there was a pleased expression on his face. That bag held the five ingredients to his next big score.

No one was home. He hurried upstairs to his room and quickly unpacked the five pieces of ware. From a distance they were identical to the five pieces on the table in the basement—all except one. That one was an original and must be put in the place of the crude duplicate he'd made and which he fervently hoped was still resting safely on the table beside the other four originals.

A little later, first making sure Mrs. Browning wasn't in sight, Baxter slipped down to the basement to substitute the original piece of ware for the poor imitation he'd placed far back on the table. His heart jumped when he saw that the pieces had been moved. He examined them carefully before he hurried back upstairs to his room. Had the kid discovered the substitution? The pieces had been moved. That could mean trouble. He'd have to be careful. He couldn't afford to have anything go wrong now. Well, he could read women like Mary Hilton and kids like Chip

Hilton like a book. He'd be able to tell by their actions when they came home.

The three hours that followed were long and anxious ones. This scheme had been so cleverly worked out and was moving along so beautifully that it would be a shame for something to screw it up now.

Baxter made sure he was in the family room when Mary Hilton arrived home. The warmth in her greeting reassured him. Now he knew it was just the kid he'd have to worry about.

Chip had gone directly to the Sugar Bowl after school and then hurried home to have a light supper before the Parkton game. He hoped Baxter hadn't returned yet. When he found him talking with his mom, his gray eyes clouded with disappointment.

Baxter was enthusiastic in his greeting, but his sharp eyes were alert and observant as he studied Chip's face when they gripped hands. He breathed a slight sigh of relief when he noted no apparent change in Chip's manner. The kid had never been too friendly, but there was no new restraint in his greeting. Baxter felt sure everything was all right. The plan was safe.

CHAPTER 16

Varsity Shake-up

COACH ROCKWELL opened the door to the Big Reds' locker room at exactly 7:30 Friday night, and the players didn't have to look up to know who it was.

Rockwell cleared his throat, waiting until every player gave him his attention. Then he began talking about Parkton.

"They're big and they fight and they work hard off the boards. They use a switching defense. That means they trade men every time an opponent crosses in front of them. They look for interceptions all the time. They play dummy most of the time until they catch you napping and making a sloppy, careless pass. Then they dart for the ball and for the interception.

"When they get the ball, they break down the floor for the little gift you were kind enough to make—the two points you just gave away. The second time that happens to one of you tonight, just start walking right over to the bench and sit down beside me.

"Now, as an offense against their defense, we'll change direction when we're in the backcourt and cut right down the middle. Instead of crossing in a weave or a roll, we'll start as if we're going to do that and then we'll change direction and cut toward the basket. Maybe one of you can drag both of the men who are getting ready to switch with you and then the other man will be free for an open shot.

"On the defense, we'll play a straight man-to-man with no switching. Each of you will be responsible for your own man."

Every player waited for Rockwell to name the usual starters: Browning, Morris, Hilton, Rodriguez, and Schwartz. But several players waited with thumping hearts, hoping this would be the night that Rock would call their names.

"Browning at center, Hilton and Schwartz up front—"

Yep. It was the same old line-up.

"Morris and Barnes at the guards! Let's go!"

They all sprang to their feet and rushed to join hands with Rockwell in a small circle. Then they followed Chip out the door, up the hall, and out onto the court. As each player passed through the door, Rockwell thumped him on the back. As each stepped down to the hall level, Pop Brown added, "Let's go!"

After Pop Brown's encouragement, each one jogged behind Chip, but they were all thinking the same thing: Rock had benched Mike Rodriguez for Brevin Barnes!

Chip was thinking Mike would be sore at him. Mike might even think he'd said something to Rock about their differences over shooting and scoring.

Speed Morris was thinking Rock had a lot of nerve to put Brevin in Mike's place. Sure, he liked Brev, but Mike was a veteran and one of their best shots.

Mike Rodriguez was bitter and was thinking just what Chip had been afraid he'd think.

Taps Browning wasn't thinking much about it. He didn't care who Rockwell put on the team just as long as he left Chip Hilton on it—and Taps Browning.

Red Schwartz was a little glad, but he wished it'd been Soapy instead of Brevin to take Mike's place. He didn't go for this, and Speed wouldn't either. What in the world was Chip thinking when he started helping Brevin at the cost of his friends?

Soapy Smith was thinking maybe it wasn't a bad idea to get someone in there in Rodriguez's place. Mike had been throwing the ball away with too many bad shots. A guy could spot bad shooting better when he was sitting on the bench. He ought to know; he had enough splinters to be an expert on the subject. Maybe Rock would give him a chance if Barnes fell down or got the measles like Speed.

Brevin Barnes was wishing this hadn't happened. He didn't want to play this badly, didn't want to take any player's place, didn't think he was good enough to start. He thought that most of the veterans, except Chip and Taps and maybe Soapy Smith, wouldn't want to team up with him since he was taking another varsity member's place.

Parkton was tough. Chip and all the other Big Reds discovered that just as soon as they got the ball and tried to penetrate the switch defense. Taps beat the Parkton center to the jump, and Chip came in high on the signal and took the ball. Then he passed to Speed and pivoted toward the right corner so the middle of the court would be open. That would make it easy for Speed and Barnes and Red to change direction and cut down the middle according to Rockwell's instructions.

But Speed didn't pass the ball to Schwartz or Barnes, didn't change direction, and didn't cut down the middle of the court. He continued with the ball, dribbling for all he was worth. He ran into a stone wall of sagging or floating Parkton players who gummed up the middle and took the ball away from him.

The Parkton switch defense was a lot like a zone when a player tried to drive through with the ball. It closed up tight. Some coaches call this method of ganging up on the man with the ball "sagging" or "floating." Rockwell maintained it was really a zone defense and that anyone who claimed he used a pure man-to-man or a switch defense and combined floating in it was inconsistent. But no matter what Parkton's defense was called, it was effective. The fact that he'd lost the ball seemed to infuriate Speed, and he bullheadedly tried it again and again.

Then Rockwell surprised every member of the squad. For the first time in three years, Speed Morris came out of a game in the first five minutes of play.

Morris was fuming when Teddy Rice came trotting out on the floor in his place. Even though Speed was a good sport at heart and tried to mask his feelings, everybody knew he was angry and hurt.

The customary Big Reds procedure was for any player who left the floor to come directly to the bench and sit down beside Rockwell. Morris never gave it a thought. He'd rarely left a game at all in the three years he'd played. Now he was angry because he hadn't been able to break through the switch defense and a little ashamed of his stubborn persistence. He forgot all about sitting down on the bench beside his coach.

Rockwell was a considerate man. He made it a personal rule to pat the exiting player on the shoulder, giving him a smile and an "OK, young man," but he never added to that greeting until the game was on again and the spectators were back to watching the game. Then he'd talk to the player, pointing out mistakes or giving instructions.

When Speed came off the court, Rockwell expected him to come directly to the vacant place on the bench. However the angry guard hurried to the extreme end of the bench, looking neither to the right nor to the left. Rockwell half rose, apparently to call Speed, but then he seemed to change his mind and, instead, motioned to Smith to sit beside him. So it was Soapy who got the instructions Rockwell had planned to give Speed Morris. Rockwell spoke in a low voice to Soapy, explaining why he'd sent Teddy Rice in to take the veteran guard's place.

"You can't dribble through their defense, Soapy. You've got to use a give-and-go offense from the backcourt, unless you pass the ball forward to the post and then cut down the middle for a return pass. Keep in mind that the strength of their defense is based upon clogging up the center of the court in front of the basket. That's why we've got Chip and Red playing out of the corners. Get it? Okay. Now relax and watch. You'll probably be in there in a couple of minutes!"

Soapy wasn't in there in a couple of minutes and neither was Speed. Teddy Rice was teaming up beautifully with Brevin Barnes in give-and-go plays that Chet Stewart had drilled into them day after day. Teddy and Brevin were clicking. First Teddy would pass to Brevin and reverse direction to receive the return pass and score. Then it would be Barnes who would work the play. It didn't take long for the home fans to get behind the two rookies.

"Look at those kids go!"

"Beats anything I ever saw!"

Up in the center of the stands, directly opposite the division line that split the middle of the court, big, happy-go-lucky Jim Rice turned to his wife and nearly submerged her with his big, wide smile. Leslie Rice was smiling, too, but she kept her eyes fixed on the kid who'd taken Morris's place. She nodded her head when Jim said Barnes was working well with Teddy, that they sure made a good combination, and that Rock was really something the way he could put his finger on the right combination.

At the half, Parkton led, 28-23, but the respectability of the score was due to the almost single-handed offensive efforts of Rice and Barnes. The Valley Falls scorebook, the official book because it was the home team's, had four *X*s behind Brevin Barnes's name in the field-goal column, and there were two *X*s in the field-goal column and one *X* in the free-throw column on the line beside Teddy Rice's name. Yes, those two had made more than half of Valley Falls's points!

When the second half began, everyone noticed Rockwell had made no change in the line-up from the end of the first half. Henry Rockwell believed in keeping a winning combination intact as long as possible. But after three minutes of second-half play, it was evident something was wrong. The give-and-go plays of the former JV captain and Brevin Barnes were no longer effective. In fact, the two had lost the ball the first three times they tried the plays that had worked so well toward the end of the first half, and Parkton was now out in front, 34-23.

Rockwell stood up, and Chip immediately called time. "Won't do, men," Rockwell said, shaking his head. "We've got to change our attack. They're not switching now. They're just standing there in front of the basket and picking off the passes we're throwing down the middle."

He turned and looked down toward the end of the bench where Speed and Mike were sitting side by side. He eyed them a moment and then beckoned Soapy and Lefty. They joined the huddle, and Rockwell patted Brevin and Teddy on the shoulders and told them to sit down. "Nice work, kids." Then he turned back to the huddle.

"Pay attention now," he barked. "Chip, you work right under the basket as you did year before last. Taps, you go to the left corner, and Red, you take the right corner. We'll play close to the baseline. Maybe that'll keep them from floating. Soapy, you and Lefty try to work the ball to the corners, either corner. And from the corners we'll try to get the ball to Chip under the basket. If we can't get it in to Chip, the opposite corner man will cut across and in front of Chip, and the player in the corner with the ball will feed the ball to this cutter. Clear? No? Well, listen . . .

"We'll suppose Red has the ball in the right corner and can't get the ball to Chip. Taps, you cut around in front of Chip and toward the ball, and then Red will try to hit you coming toward the basket. Clear? Good!

"Now, suppose Red can't pass to Chip under the basket and he can't get the ball to Taps cutting across. Just as soon as Taps passes you, Chip, you back up to the free-throw line. Then, Red, you feed Chip the ball with a quick, hard pass. And, Chip, I want you to shoot every time you get the ball, no matter where that happens to be—near the basket, at the free-throw line, or behind the three-point line! That's an order! Now—"

The horn sounded just then, and Rockwell gestured impatiently toward the scorer's table. He pushed Chip toward the referee standing with the ball just outside their huddle. "Tell him we want another full time-out, Chip!"

Chip called the second consecutive one-minute time-out, and as soon as he rejoined the huddle, Rockwell continued.

"Now, Chip and Taps and Red, I want you three to hit the boards on every shot and keep putting that ball back up."

Rockwell turned to Soapy Smith and jabbed a hard forefinger at his chest. "You," he said harshly, "you used to have a good shot. So, every time your guard drops back toward the basket, I want you to fire at that hoop. Red or Taps or Chip will get you the ball. Let's go in there and do it and win this game! Report, Soapy! You, too, Lefty!"

For the next five minutes it looked as though Rockwell's revised attack might work. Chip scored every point the Big Reds made in the next five minutes—six straight goals in ten shots. At the end of the third quarter the score was Parkton 40, Valley Falls 35.

When the fourth quarter started, every Valley Falls basketball fan realized Parkton was concentrating on stopping Chip Hilton. They double-teamed him, blocked him away from the basket, fouled him, and did everything but tie him up with a rope. Those tactics cut down on his scoring effectiveness, all right, but Chip passed off time and again to Red and Soapy when two Parkton players shifted to stop his shots. But Red's shooting was off, and Soapy couldn't seem to come close.

Even at that, Chip got eight points—one field goal and six free throws. But the rest of the Big Reds only scored five points, and that wasn't quite enough. Parkton held on to win 50-48, handing Valley Falls their third straight defeat.

Once again, the passengers in Speed's Mustang were ill at ease and aware of that new strangeness that was making conversation difficult. Speed was hurt and quiet, and Chip didn't know what to say. Irrepressible Soapy, however, couldn't be stilled and reproached Speed for not sitting down beside Rockwell when he came out of the game.

"But, Soapy," Speed remonstrated, "I forgot all about it! It never entered my mind!"

"That's easy to understand," Chip said quickly. "Speed's always played almost every minute of every game. Anyone could make that mistake."

"Yeah, sure," Biggie Cohen drawled, "but we'd have won that game if Speed hadn't overlooked the fact that Rock might have wanted to share a little information with him. Plus, I don't think Rock felt very good about the way Mike was sulking."

Speed nodded his head in self-reproach. "What an idiot I am," he groaned. "I would sit down there beside Mike. Man, Rock probably thinks I was sulking too!"

CHAPTER 17

Biggie Takes Charge

SUNDAY HAD always been a special day at the Hiltons, and Chip looked forward to it all week. The everyday grind of school, practice, work, and study took a lot out of him. Sunday was also the only day he and his mom had to spend together.

Before Baxter's arrival, Sunday was for late sleeping, late breakfast, leisurely reading of the newspapers, church, 2:00 dinner, and the gathering of the members of the Hilton A. C. at any time but always by 3:00. The guys would raid the refrigerator at 5:00 and then hang out until snacks at 7:00. Then Chip hit the books.

Taps Browning had a part in most of the Sunday routine—even crawling into the extra bed in Chip's room more often than he crawled into his own next door. Soapy Smith's presence was taken for granted. He was just as likely to turn up at 8:00 in the morning as 7:00 at night.

But regular as a clock, he always made his appearance in time for his 2:00 feeding, reluctantly permitting himself to be escorted to the table. As Soapy himself said, he was an epicure.

Sunday's at Hiltons' had been a tradition for years—until T. A. K. Baxter maneuvered himself into the middle of things. Then, little by little, the routine changed. Taps began to stay home more often, Soapy didn't show up quite so early or stay so long, and the other members of the crowd began to appear less frequently. Chip didn't like it, but Mary Hilton, charmed by Baxter's glib stories of Big Chip Hilton, didn't even notice the change.

When Chip came downstairs the Sunday morning after the Parkton game, his mom and Baxter were in the family room reading the papers. Baxter greeted Chip cordially and held out the *Times*.

"Says here you're back in stride again," he said. "Saw the game myself and thought you were splendid. Here, read the story."

Mary Hilton interrupted. "Yes, Chip, and read the story on the front page too. We're going to lose Mr. Baxter very soon. He's going to England!"

The glance Chip turned toward Baxter was questioning, but it was hopeful too. Baxter read the glance correctly, and his mouth twitched with a little smile.

"Yes," he said, stroking the small, graying mustache, "I'm afraid I'll have to leave your beautiful little town, Chip, in a week or so. Probably the week following our game."

He smiled again and added, "People will probably run me out of town after you high schoolers give my Independents a shellacking!"

Mrs. Hilton pointed to the front page of the paper. "It says in the *Post* that Mr. Baxter is being sent to England by the Gately Pottery Company to make arrangements for the purchase of five million dollars worth of English clay."

"That's right," Baxter said modestly, "and then I'm going to spend a couple of months in Europe and rest up. Writing a book isn't as easy as a lot of people think, especially if it's concerned with a technical subject."

"Is the book nearly finished?" Mary Hilton asked.

Baxter assured her it was and then went into a long discourse about his new discoveries in the field of ceramics and how he hoped to use them to revolutionize American methods of producing pottery.

Chip welcomed this opportunity to escape to the lab, taking the paper and Hoops with him. He unlocked the door and sat down to read what Joe Kennedy had to say about the game.

Times and Sports
by Joe Kennedy

Valley Falls's state champs lost their third straight game last night. Rockwell's veterans, with the exception of Chip Hilton, seem to be skidding fast. The return of Hilton's shooting eye was the only redeeming feature of a dull contest.

Is Mike Rodriguez definitely shelved? Are reports that he turned in his uniform last night authentic? Rockwell didn't use Rodriguez at all last night. And what's wrong with Speed Morris? He played only the first few minutes. Can't still be measles.

What's happened to the scoring of Schwartz, Browning, and Morris? Seems that as Chip Hilton goes, so go the Big Reds. When he doesn't score, the game isn't even close. Parkton gave Hilton the works last night, but he still hit for 20 points.

Teddy Rice, former JV captain, played a good second quarter and so did his JV teammate, Brevin Barnes. These youngsters show plenty of promise, but they still need more game experience.

The Big Reds - Independents game—benefiting the Damon Runyon Cancer Fund—scheduled for Saturday, January 25, is sold out. The school's seating capacity could be doubled and would still be inadequate to handle the fans who want to see the game.

The Independents are favored—more experience and bigger. Five scorers—Kelly, Dobson, Strickland, Spears, and Moore—are all expert marksmen. They can really scorch the nets.

This intracity contest may mark the last appearance of T. A. K. Baxter as coach of the Independents. He leaves for England shortly to purchase clay for a big domestic consortium. Baxter's chemical discoveries may revolutionize American pottery methods.

Hope you have your ticket for the Cancer Fund game.

Chip tossed the paper on the table and breathed a sigh of relief. So Baxter *was* leaving. It couldn't be soon enough for Chip.

He picked up one of the five pieces of pottery and his thoughts went back to the rough piece. He examined each one carefully and was surprised to find they were almost identical. The rough piece seemed to have disappeared. Maybe he'd imagined it! No, it had been real enough. He examined each of the pieces again. No, they were all alike. Each was as smooth and perfect in balance and weight as the others. He couldn't have dreamed it! "Hoops, sure wish you could talk; then I'd know what's going on around here." Hoops, a typical cat, wandered out of the lab and upstairs for a nap.

While Chip was in the lab, Biggie Cohen was at the Sugar Bowl talking to Soapy Smith. Biggie didn't like the way things were going with the team, and he didn't like the way things were going with Soapy, Speed, Mike, Red, and Chip Hilton. He'd decided to do something about it.

Soapy was first on Biggie's list, and he was glad to find the genial clown alone in the Sugar Bowl. Biggie lowered himself gingerly into a seat at one of the tables and shook a massive finger toward Soapy, who was leaning forward with his elbows on the top of the counter.

"Look, my friend," Biggie began, "you and I have to have a little understanding. You're one of the chief reasons this ball club of ours is crashing on the rocks!"

Soapy's eyes opened wide with surprise, and he straightened up with genuine amazement. "Me? Me?"

"Yes, you! You're one of the chief offenders. And Speed's another, and Mike is another, and Red's another—"

Soapy's mouth opened wide and his lower lip dropped in astonishment. "Are you out of your mind?" he managed.

Then Biggie let him have it. No, he wasn't out of his mind! But Soapy Smith was! Soapy Smith and Speed Morris and Mike Rodriguez and Red Schwartz.

The team had been rolling until everyone began to go shot crazy! It was no longer a team—it was a bunch of selfish, hotshot gunners. And all because a bunch of pickup, run-down has-beens known as the Valley Falls Independents were beating a few other no-name basketball teams. The Big Reds, he accused, now needed four or five balls to play.

It was all because Soapy and the rest of them had fallen for a showboat who'd played basketball before the

Titanic went down and who'd mesmerized just about every person in town because he could shoot a basketball—unguarded. Big Deal!

So the best team in the state begins to look like elementary material, and Rock has to bring up a couple of kindergartners to bolster a team that should beat any high school in the country . . .

There was more, and it was backed up by 230 pounds of fighting spirit. Soapy Smith took it all in—and liked it. After Biggie Cohen stalked out of the Sugar Bowl on the prowl for Speed Morris, Mike Rodriguez, and Red Schwartz, a redheaded teenager who'd never been very serious about anything except eating and sports stood there so long and so quietly that Petey Jackson figured he was sick.

But Soapy wasn't sick. He was thinking what fools they'd been! Chip had tried to reason with them and had sacrificed his own scoring to prove he didn't want the headlines as Mike Rodriguez had claimed.

Soapy was sorry about Mike. He was a pretty good guy, but he was undependable and always seemed to be in trouble. Last year, right in the stretch when every player was needed, Rockwell had been forced to drop him from the squad for breaking training.

Soapy banged a fist so hard on the fountain it hurt. He resolved "startin' right now" to do his part to get the team back on track and to end the hard feelings between the guys. Biggie Cohen had been right!

Biggie didn't do quite so well with Mike Rodriguez. Mike was adamant. No, he was through and that was that! He'd already turned in his uniform and he wasn't going back even if Rockwell begged!

"But you quit!" Biggie reminded him. "Rock didn't tell you to turn in your uniform!"

"Yeah, but he benched me, didn't he? Benched me for a JV, didn't he? He dissed me, didn't he?"

Biggie talked to Mike for over an hour, trying to explain that Rock was probably right in benching him. He'd been taking wild shots and had dropped his team play. He was undoubtedly one of the best shooters in the state, and Rock had depended upon him to break up the sagging and zone defenses. But it was useless to talk to Mike. He'd made up his mind. Mike settled everything with his parting declaration.

"Look, Biggie," he said, "I've joined the Independents. Coach Baxter asked me to report for practice Monday night. I'm through with Rock, the Big Reds, and playing second string to the great Chip Hilton!"

That was enough for Biggie Cohen. He turned away without another word and started for Speed Morris's house. Biggie was down, but determined to see it through. He found Speed at home. Red Schwartz was there too. So was Speed's father. One look at the two Morrises and Biggie knew Mr. Morris was in the middle of a tirade. That was bad news for a young man by the name of Robert "Speed" Morris.

Robert "Bull" Morris was as tall as Biggie and thirty pounds heavier. He was a lawyer who'd gained his nickname from his college football days as a formidable lineman. Attorneys across the courtroom aisle respected him and felt his nickname was still most appropriate. Mr. Morris smiled a greeting at Biggie and then turned back to Speed just as if they were alone. He proceeded to tell Speed just about what Biggie had planned to tell him.

"The first game I've seen this year and you looked like you'd never played basketball. No wonder Rockwell took you out of the game. I'd have sent you home! I'm going to see that game Saturday night and, believe me, you better play the way you can play." He gestured toward the door. "Now, beat it! All three of you!"

Speed was relieved to get out of the house and so was Red. Biggie was still chuckling when they turned the corner and started down Main Street. Schwartz wiped his forehead with his coat sleeve. "Wow!" he muttered grimly, "I felt like I was guilty and about to be sentenced."

Speed agreed. "I know the feeling. Believe me! I must've been terrible!"

Biggie acted like Mr. Morris's junior partner. He agreed Speed had been terrible, all right, then Biggie carried right on where Speed's father had left off. He did it so well that when the three friends reached the Sugar Bowl, they stopped outside long enough to grip hands and eye one another with an expression that promised bad news for Valley Falls High School's future opponents—but good news for one Chip Hilton.

CHAPTER 18

Star on the Bench

THE CHIEF topic of conversation in the cafeteria Monday was basketball. Mike Rodriguez was the object of the greatest interest. He'd told everybody he'd quit the team and would play with the Independents Saturday night "on a team where every player has a chance to score and for a coach who doesn't play favorites!"

That didn't go over well with the Big Reds fans. Still, some of the students, disgruntled over three consecutive defeats, sided with Rodriguez on some of the things he was saying. One or two Big Reds regulars heard it, too, and so did Chip. But he'd always liked Mike, and he ignored the bluster.

Rockwell got a surprise that afternoon. In fact, it was almost a shock. The Big Reds tore into practice with an eagerness and a passion that reminded him of the spirit the previous year's team had shown in its drive to the championship. That drive and pep carried over to practice on Tuesday and continued at the Weston game in which Chip Hilton starred by scoring twenty-five points, making the clutch basket with only five seconds to play when the Big Reds were one point behind.

Rockwell was still passing up Speed and sent Chip, Taps, Soapy, Red, and Brevin out on the floor to start the game. He remained steadfast even when Weston forged ahead and held the lead right down to the last five seconds. Rockwell knew Morris and Rodriguez were close friends, and he was determined to break up the individualism that had ruined the Big Reds' team play, even if it meant he had to lose every game.

So Speed sat out, sat out for thirty-two minutes. For the first time since entering Valley Falls High School, he sat on the bench for an entire game and watched someone else play. Nonetheless, he was cheering all the way, and his heart leaped as high as it could leap when Chip made that last-second bucket to win the game for Valley Falls, 56-55.

When the horn sounded, the bench exploded onto the court and lit all over Chip, playfully rubbing his head, hugging his neck, and jumping on his shoulders. Speed Morris led the charge.

The Big Reds liked afternoon games because they got home early and had a chance to play them all over again at the Sugar Bowl. The game with Weston had started at 4:00, and by 6:00 the Big Reds had snapped out of their losing streak, showered, and were in the bus singing songs, wisecracking, and cheering one another as though they'd won the state championship.

Soapy, standing in the front of the bus, acted as master of ceremonies and led the cheering. "All right, now," he shouted, "let's have one for Brevin—"

"Yea, Brevin—Yea, Barnes—Yea, Brevin Barnes!"

Soapy applauded the cheer and then hollered, "Now, how about one for—" He twisted his head to look back at Rockwell sitting right behind the driver. Then he cupped his hands and whispered hoarsely, "Let's have one for cement head—"

The yell that followed Soapy's lead was a bit raucous, but the cheer sounded good to Rockwell.

"Yea, Coach—Yea, Rockwell—Yea, Coach Rockwell!"

Soapy hooked a thumb at Chet Stewart. "How about a big one for the worry wart?"

"Yea, Coach—Yea, Stewart—Yea, Coach Stewart!"

"How about one for the Independents?" Bill English baited.

That didn't stump Soapy. "OK, guys, let's have a big Bronx cheer!"

"How about one for the twenty-five-point man?"

"Yea, Chip—Yea, Hilton—Yea, Chip Hilton!"

When they tired of cheering, Soapy led the singing. Rockwell listened to the off-key chorus of happy, young voices and his heart began to glow so much it hurt. That old lump popped up in his throat again.

"The greatest job in the world," he muttered.

Chet Stewart leaned closer. "What did you say?" he asked.

Rockwell shook his head and smiled. "I said it's good to win one! Best feeling in the world!"

The Thursday papers should've given ink to a familiar headline "Big Reds Win!" but they didn't. Oh, they gave the usual report of the game and the box score, but there were no lengthy columns by Pete Williams and Joe

Kennedy. "The greatest game in the history of basketball" was to be played in Valley Falls Saturday night, and the newspapers—front page, back page, social page, business page, and sports page—all gave the "Independents-Big Reds" game more space than they'd given the Big Reds the year before when they'd won the state championship.

The Independents were favored by almost everyone, especially by Jerry Davis and his clique. They figured the game was a good opportunity to renew their assault on Rockwell. They were sure Baxter and his liberal style of basketball would be too much for Rockwell and his conservative methods.

Most of the older hoop fans thought the Independents were a cinch, too, but there were a few diehards, like John Schroeder, Bull Morris, and Jim Rice, who believed in the kids and in Henry Rockwell.

Chip had been a three-letter man ever since he'd entered high school. Now a senior, he was well on his way to making it a grand slam. He'd earned his letter each year either as a player or as a manager. During those years and in all the accompanying practices and games, he'd learned to recognize most of his coach's moods. But he couldn't figure out the Rockwell who was so cool and impersonal at Thursday's practice. The coach said nothing at all about the victory at Weston or about the upcoming Cancer Fund game. Rockwell worked the team briefly on freezing the ball and meeting a pressing defense, and then dismissed practice.

Friday's practice, however, found a different coach on the job. His movements were quick and his voice brittle and sharp as he directed them through the practice.

Chip knew this was the Rockwell who'd led Valley Falls to the championship of the state, the Rockwell who'd been able to devote his time to scouting and to preparing his team to meet the attacks and the defenses they'd need against their opponents—instead of using every minute of his time keeping peace among his own players.

Rockwell waved the players toward the bleachers as Pop Brown rolled the board over. One by one, Rockwell wrote the names of the starting five for the Independents and discussed each in such detail that every listener was amazed.

Where had the Rock gotten all this?

He had them scoped to the last little detail.

Say, the Rock was different. He meant business!

"Dobson is their center. Naturally, in their attack there is no center, no forwards, and no guards. Every player is a forward and every player is a guard—what little guarding they do.

"A pressing attack is simply a constant advance toward the basket with little or no thought to playing defense. The pressing principle is designed to cause the opponent to make mistakes, mistakes like attempting a cross-court pass or pivoting away from a teammate so they can double up on you. Keep in mind that they're constantly advancing toward their own basket. They're not interested in retreating. They don't care how many points you make just as long as they make one more or are one point ahead when the game is over. That's why the style of play isn't sound. That's why you're going to beat them and beat them bad!"

Rockwell paused and flashed a sharp look at each player. There was determination in the set of his chin and everyone knew what that meant—Rock was primed.

"Now back to Dobson! He's so slow he couldn't catch a cold. They use him only to grab the rebounds if you miss or to take the ball out of the net if you score. Then he's supposed to fire it upcourt to one of the other four who drive in for the score. The sole idea is to outnumber you and drive in for the score. If you stop their drives, they throw the ball back out for those three-pointers. Lots of times Dobson is down under the opponent's basket all alone and that's another weakness! I'll cover that later.

"Chip, you'll be playing against Dobson. Taps, you won't start this game. Sorry, but I know you're more interested in the team's winning than you are in playing. Not that you won't get in the game! But Chip is faster and can do just what we have to do to break the back of their attack. I'll talk to you about that later, Chip.

"Strickland is just an over-the-hill man trying to relive high school days when he weighed 140 instead of 240! Lefty, you'll be playing him. You're ten times as fast, and I want you to be all over him all the time.

"Spears is a pretty fair ballplayer. He's still in shape and likes to play. Red, he's your problem. He goes to his right all the time, and he couldn't make a left-handed shot if his life depended upon it! You overshift all night on him and force him to go to his left! Get it?

"Moore gets all his points under the basket. He couldn't throw it in the Pacific if he was ten feet from shore. That means your job, Soapy, is to block him out. Block him away from the basket all night.

"That brings us to Kelly, the spearhead of the Independents' attack. He's what we used to call a cherry picker when I played. Doesn't play defense, just stays near his basket waiting for the long pass and an easy score. That's why he makes so many points. That means that to prevent his easy scores, one of our backcourt players will have to take him and stay with him even when we have the ball. Barnes, you play Kelly!"

Rockwell paused. In the tight little silence that followed, every player in the bleachers got the significance of the starting line-up Rockwell had just announced.

Morris wasn't going to start.

Benched for two in a row.

Last year's captain and an All-State forward!

Maybe he'd quit like Mike.

Rockwell tapped the board with the marker, his way of getting absolute attention.

"As most of you know, this team has been going downhill and I've been forced to make several changes. So far, the changes have been for the best. Frankly, I'm very happy about the spirit you've shown this week, and if you keep it up, you'll be the team you should have been.

"Now benching a regular is a hard thing to do, but a coach has to make the changes he thinks are best for the team, not for the individual. Taps, here, has to ride the bench tomorrow night for a while, maybe for the whole game. But I know Taps feels the way I do, feels the team comes first. I'm not worried about Taps getting upset and turning in his uniform. I know he's not that kind of person.

"Maybe some of you are wondering why I benched Mike and Speed. Well, this ball club wasn't going any place, fast! I benched those two because all of our trouble, offensively, came from the backcourt. The backcourt players control a team's attack. Mike and Speed completely forgot about our style of team play that had been so effective. They began to try to score from long range, which threw our whole plan of attack out of gear.

"Mike, as you all know, has joined the Independents. I'm sorry Mike did that. I realize how tough it is to sit the bench after you've been a regular. It takes real courage to keep smiling and cheering your teammates when you know in your heart you're one of the best players on the squad.

"But there comes a time in every athlete's life when he has to bench himself through a realization of his mistakes—or the coach has to do it for him. Sometimes a player benches himself because he forgets all about the team and gets wrapped up in himself too much. Often a player is sent to the sidelines because of an injury or because a better man comes along. And sometimes a player has to be benched for the good of the team. That's the coach's responsibility. It's tough, but it has to be done.

"Speed is one of the greatest athletes I've ever coached. I don't mind saying that to his face. It's true, and I'm sure he knows I feel that way about him. But Speed forgot for a little while about the team. I've been watching him for the past couple weeks and—"

Rockwell's crooked smile flashed across his face for a second and then was gone.

"And what I've seen I've liked. The athlete who stays on his toes while sitting on the bench is hard to keep off the floor!"

CHAPTER 19

Teamwork Does It

CARS WERE parked in every inch of space for blocks around the Valley Falls High School gym. The parking lot beside Ohlsen Stadium was packed, and attendants were waving and telling drivers to keep going. People stood at the bottom of the long flight of steps leading to the gym, and two to three hundred or more were jammed against the entrance waiting for the doors to open.

In the locker room, Rockwell was standing in the corner, one foot on a chair, watching and waiting for the team to get dressed and be seated on the long bench facing the board. While he stood there, his thoughts were just a little bitter. Every player, every student, and every fan in Valley Falls seemed to have forgotten that the Big Reds were fighting to hold their championship honors, to say nothing of the leadership of Section Two.

This Independents game had even overshadowed the traditional fight with Steeltown, which would take place next Wednesday. What in the world had hit all these hundreds of people? Even now they were crowding into the building, pushing and elbowing to get in to watch a high school team play a pickup team of wanna-be basketball players. They must be crazy. Hoop crazy! It was beyond him. But one thing was sure—everyone else may have forgotten about the race or sectional and state honors, but he hadn't. Not by a long shot. He studied the kids' faces and smiled with satisfaction. They were ready for this game, all right. Ready with their plays and their fight, and ready with the most important thing of all: team spirit!

Rockwell didn't waste any time on pregame instructions. He'd taken care of that the evening before. When he said, "Let's go," there was the usual team circle of hands, joining as one, followed by a strong and proud, "Go Big Reds!" Then they formed a line facing the door, with Chip in the lead, holding the ball. Rockwell walked to the door, opened it, and away they went, crowding and stepping on the heels of the teammate in front in their rush to "get at 'em!"

Chip pushed through the overflowing crowd and saw that the Independents were already practicing. When he dashed onto the floor and dribbled hard for the basket, the stands rose as one and a roar filled the gym.

As Chip trotted back up the court for the layup line, he glanced at the other bench. Baxter was standing right on the court as though he were afraid someone in that great crowd wouldn't see him. Then Chip saw Mike Rodriguez taking long three-pointers at the other end of the court. It still didn't seem right for Mike to be playing on a team against the Big Reds.

A few minutes later, the referee was out in the middle of the center circle holding the ball, and Chip and his starting teammates huddled with Rockwell for a last-second "Let's go!"

Every player on the Big Reds' bench was standing, clapping hands, and yelling. Up in the stands, next to Suzy Browning and her parents, Mrs. Hilton stood, her eyes fixed on her son, the captain of the Valley Falls High School team.

Chip lined up just outside the jump circle and eyed Dobson. Bob Dobson was six-five, heavily muscled, and, just as Rockwell said, he looked slow. The two players shook hands as the other starters of the two teams jockeyed for positions around the circle, and then the ball was in the air. Chip leaped with the toss, and the Big Reds had the ball.

The crowd's cheering was one long, continuous roar as Schwartz controlled the tap. Red pivoted with the ball and saw Chip cutting to the basket. Schwartz hit Chip with a perfect pass for an easy layup. The Big Reds were out in front by two points.

The fans shrieked as they waited for the Independents' famed fast break, but nothing happened. Dobson had followed Chip too late to stop the score, but he grabbed the ball as it dropped through the net and stepped out of bounds to fire a long one upcourt. But he noticed something was wrong. It was Chip Hilton. Chip was dancing up and down in front of him, waving his arms and kicking his feet, and, up the court, Brevin Barnes was right behind Joe Kelly, while Lefty Peters was swarming all over Pete Strickland. Dobson ran toward the corner, still holding the ball, and the referee blew his whistle. Violation! Dobson had held the ball out of bounds for more than five seconds. Turnover!

Before Dobson knew what had happened, Chip wrestled the ball out of his hands, handed it to the referee, and stepped out of bounds. The official returned the ball, and Chip rifled it to Lefty Peters who cut like a streak for the basket, and the kids had scored again. This time Dobson didn't get the ball before it hit the floor, and the official had to pick it up and hand it to him. But Chip wasn't asleep, and just as Dobson caught the ball, Chip rushed in front of him as before, waving his hands and kicking his feet. This time Dobson was fearful of another five-second call, and so he threw the ball as hard as he could toward Moore, who was hanging under the Independents' basket. But the ball never reached him. Soapy had been sticking to Moore like a leech. When he saw the long pass coming, he left him like a shot, leaped high in the air, intercepted the pass, and fired it right back to Chip.

It was a long pass. Chip pivoted with the catch and drove in to the basket for the layup. Dobson chased him, and just as Chip released the ball, he hit Chip's arm and it was a three-point play. The scoreboard flickered twice when the referee raised two fingers. Then when Chip dropped the free throw through the ring, it flickered again, and the scoreboard showed: Home 7, Visitors 0.

Captain Bill Spears called for a time-out, and the crowd's roar died down to a jumbled babble of astonishment as the fans gazed at the scoreboard in shocked surprise. The kids had scored seven points in less than two minutes.

Chip, in the huddle with the guys and Rockwell, was facing the Independents' bench and could see Baxter nodding in his direction. He looked down quickly and concentrated on Rockwell's words.

"Nice going! You're playing it just right! Don't do anything different. Just keep it up! All right, Chip? Soapy? Red? OK, Lefty? Brevin? Good! Stay right on top of them now! Let's go!"

The Big Reds kept on top of them, all right. Not once did the famed fast break work, and the Independents' three-point prowess boomeranged because the kids rushed their older opponents every second, causing their shots to become bricks, clanks, and airballs rather than controlled scores. It was no contest. At the end of the quarter the Big Reds led, 19-10, and at the half the score was Valley Falls 37, Independents 20. Chip had scored sixteen points on six baskets and four free throws.

Rockwell was grimly proud of his kids when he followed them into the locker room. Still, he followed the usual between-half procedure to the letter and then sent them back to finish the job with instructions to keep right on using the same tactics.

"Keep on top of them. Give them a dose of their own medicine. They can't handle it, and they don't like it, and they can't do a thing about it! Make them play your game!"

Rockwell was only partly right. The Independents couldn't handle it and they didn't like it, but they had decided to do something about it—and that something was to get physical with Chip Hilton. Dobson started it right off the bat. On the throw-in beginning the third quarter, he leaped forward and upward and jabbed his left elbow into Chip's stomach. Dobson didn't mind the foul being called.

Several plays later, Red intercepted a pass and fired it to Chip, but just as Chip reached for the ball, he was sandwiched by Dobson and Spears with such a vicious crash that he was knocked sprawling to the floor.

Chip didn't like this new style of play, and he glanced at the Independents' bench to catch Baxter smiling and Mike Rodriguez and the other reserves laughing boisterously. His temper nearly got the best of him, but he fought it down.

As the game wore on and Rockwell kept the same five starters, the pace began to tell on the Independents' stamina and tempers. Time and again Chip was elbowed, hipped, blocked, and even punched in the ribs once or twice. It was hard to keep control of his temper, but he did. He wanted to play in every minute of this game and beat Baxter and his team as soundly as possible.

In the fourth quarter with five minutes left to play, the Big Reds led, 58-30. The Independents had called a time-out, and it was then that Baxter sent Mike Rodriguez in for Kelly. Long before this, the crowd had conceded the game to the Big Reds, but they half wished the Independents might break loose with their rapid-fire, high-scoring attack and make the game a little closer.

During the time-out, however, someone realized Chip Hilton had made a lot of points, and the news spread through the crowd and created a new interest. Someone announced that Hilton had not made a field goal in the second half, and a second later someone stated he'd iced sixteen consecutive free throws during the game.

"Nine buckets and sixteen free throws! Wow!"

"That's thirty-four points!"

"The high school record's thirty-nine!"

"Yeah, Bill Hilton, Chip's dad, set that record twenty-five years ago!"

"Sure of that?"

"Bill Peters said so. Played in the game with him when he set the record!"

"Pete Williams had that in his column a couple months ago!"

"I heard Stan Gomez say it on the radio a couple weeks ago!"

"Five minutes left. He might tie it!"

"I say he can't do it!"

"Can if he gets the ball."

Mary Hilton heard all those remarks and smiled. If only Chip could do what all these people seemed to want him to do—break his father's record. Bill would have liked that.

When play resumed, Mike Rodriguez lined up in place of Joe Kelly, and Brevin Barnes, who'd been playing against Kelly, extended his hand and smiled. Rodriguez turned abruptly away and ignored the hand. Then the ball was in play, and there was a new crowd reaction. Chip didn't get it at first, but his teammates got it, all right.

"Thirty-four! Thirty-four! Thirty-four!"

Chip was fouled again, and the cheer that went up drowned out the scorer's horn and everything except the shout that had now become a chant.

"Thirty-five! Thirty-five! Thirty-five!"

Chip was thinking about that "thirty-five" and nearly missed the toss, but it bounced around on the rim a couple of times and then dropped through for his thirty-fifth point. Then Chip got it! It was the record.

They wanted him to break the record—his father's record.

"Thirty-six! Thirty-six! Thirty-six!"

Spears grabbed the ball just as it dropped through the net and Chip rushed to cover the inbound pass. But he was a second too late, and Spears hooked the ball safely to Rodriguez. Mike pivoted smack into Brevin, who had followed him and tied him up.

"Thirty-six! Thirty-six! Thirty-six!"

The referee's whistle shrilled through the chant and ended the wrestling for the ball. The possession arrow pointed to Valley Falls. Mike's frustration showed when Valley Falls inbounded the ball. He jumped into Barnes using the same elbow trick Dobson had used on Chip.

The referee caught it just as he'd caught it before and called the foul. With the Independents' tenth foul of the half, Valley Falls would be awarded the bonus toss whether or not the first free throw was successful.

"Thirty-six! Thirty-six! Thirty-six!"

"Give it to Hilton! Give Hilton the ball!"

Barnes walked to the free-throw line and bounced the ball three times as he eyed the basket. Rodriguez, standing behind Barnes at the junction of the free-throw circle and the three-point line, said something that caused Brevin to miss both free throws.

"Give it to Hilton! Give it to Hilton! Give it to Hilton!"

Chip couldn't believe he'd heard Mike correctly, but even before Bill Spears could get the rebounded ball up-court, Mike said it again. And it wasn't nice. The Valley Falls captain turned toward Rodriguez in amazement. But now the crowd was chanting again.

"Thirty-six! Thirty-six! Thirty-six!"

"Give it to Hilton! Give Hilton the ball!"

Brevin followed Rodriguez to cover him on the pass from Spears, but Rodriguez either lost his head completely or believed Barnes was following him in reprisal for what he'd said, because he turned suddenly and struck Barnes full in the mouth. Brevin staggered back and went down on one knee, hardly knowing what had happened. The official immediately disqualified Rodriguez.

There was pandemonium. In an instant the floor was swarming with irate fans. Bert Rodriguez, Mike's father, rushed at Barnes and gave the boy a shove that nearly sent him down to the floor. Brevin made no effort to protect himself but stood there holding both hands to his mouth while the blood trickled through his fingers.

Before Chip could reach Brevin's side, the crowd around the youngster parted as if turned aside by two giant snowplows. Bull Morris and Jim Rice reached Brevin Barnes's side. Bert Rodriguez was still trying to get at Barnes, but Rice grabbed him and turned him around as easily as you spin a turnstile and shoved him clear off the court.

The Big Reds and Henry Rockwell walked Brevin back to their bench. Teddy Rice had been the first from the bench to run to his friend, just as his father and Mr. Morris had from the bleachers.

When the floor cleared, Principal Zimmerman used the sound system to announce the game would continue but that it would be called off immediately if there was any recurrence of the disgraceful sportsmanship displayed by some of the spectators. The crowd cheered.

This time Brevin walked to the free-throw line, bounced the ball exactly three times, and each time the ball swished cleanly through the net. The horn sounded, and when Speed Morris came trotting out on the floor to replace Barnes, the stocky star got a resounding cheer. When Brevin Barnes left the court, the crowd stood and applauded him every step of the way and long after he'd passed from sight. Then the chant was back.

"Thirty-six! Thirty-six! Thirty-six!"

The game was a mad scramble now—just the sort of a game Speed Morris liked. He was expert at intercepting bad passes, and this type of game was right down his alley. He stole the inbound pass right in front of the Big Reds' basket. One long step would have carried him under the hoop for a sure two-pointer, but he pivoted and burned the ball to Chip who was driving in from the corner. Chip banked it against the board for his thirty-seventh point.

"Thirty-eight! Thirty-eight! Thirty-eight!"

Spears took the ball out of bounds, glancing at the clock as he stepped across the line. There were eleven

TEAMWORK DOES IT

seconds left to play, and he used all he could before throwing the ball far down the court. But Soapy was ready. He picked the ball out of the air and rifled it right back to Speed down by the Big Reds' basket. Again, Speed pivoted, faked a shot, and lobbed a perfect lead pass to Chip, who'd started in to follow the shot. Just as Chip jammed the ball through the basket, Spears crashed into him head-on, and the contact spilled them both to the floor. The twenty-five-year record was tied on a slam dunk!

The stands erupted with cheers, high-fives, and dancing feet! There was so much noise that not a single person heard the official's whistle just before the horn sounded ending the game. Players and spectators swarmed out onto the floor to congratulate Chip. Finally, the frantic tooting of the referee's whistle halted them, and they saw the referee leading Chip to the free-throw line.

The announcer urged the crowd to clear the court. "Please take your seats! The game is not over! Hilton was fouled on that last play and has one free throw coming! Move back from the basket, please! Hilton has now scored thirty-nine points!"

The crowd moved away from the basket willingly enough, but that was as far as they'd go. It was an amazing spectacle. There must have been a thousand people on the floor when the referee finally gave the ball to Chip for the shot and the opportunity to set a new record. It was the most difficult play in Chip's life, and he'd never felt so nervous. To make it worse, the crowd took up the chant again.

"Forty! Forty! Forty! Forty!"

Mrs. Hilton and the Brownings hadn't moved. They'd remained standing while the crowd clambered down over the seats to the floor. Mary Hilton was holding her hands over her ears to still the deafening noise, but her eyes were watching every move Chip made. When Chip stepped to the line, arranged his feet just so, and eyed the basket, Mary Hilton breathed a little prayer and closed her eyes.

Chip's mom was probably the only person in that building who didn't see Chip sink the basket to set a new Valley Falls High School record of forty points.

CHAPTER 20

Play It Smart

PETEY JACKSON was feeling down Sunday morning after the Independents game. He'd opened the Sugar Bowl at 11:00, and at 12:30 there still hadn't been a single customer. He glanced through the front door at the driving snow that was falling so heavily it obscured the other side of the street. What a rotten day!

It wasn't the weather that had Petey down; it was T. A. K. Baxter. Petey was thoroughly disillusioned about Baxter—not because the Big Reds had defeated Baxter's Independents nor because the "great" man had neglected to pay his bill at the Sugar Bowl, leaving Petey to pay it.

Petey was both sad and disgusted because he'd believed implicitly in Baxter's style of play, especially the stories Baxter told about his basketball exploits at State. All of Petey's confidence in Baxter had been swept away even before the game when a letter arrived Saturday morning. It was signed by Robin Jennings, the sports information director at State.

HOOP CRAZY

T. A. K. Baxter had played freshman basketball at State but had never made the varsity. He'd graduated from the university twenty-three years ago. He played no other sport according to the records in the athletic department.

It was Baxter's boastful spirit that had led Petey to write to the university. Baxter's ego was so inflated he could never be satisfied with a modest athletic achievement. He had to be the hero of hundreds of outstanding feats. He'd told Petey so many stories of his great years as an athlete at State that Petey had thought he'd create a list of them to spring on Chip, Biggie, Taps, and some of the other guys who didn't care for Baxter.

Petey had brooded all day Saturday about that letter. Baxter was bogus! All his stories were lies. Why would a grown man want to lie like that? Why would anyone want to lie about his athletic ability?

Petey Jackson had been one of the first hoop fans in town to buy a ticket to the Cancer Fund game. He'd wanted to be directly behind the Independents' bench so he could watch Baxter's bench strategy. But after the letter, he didn't even feel like going to the game. As game time approached, however, his curiosity won out, and when the game started, Petey was there.

Petey muttered something and went back to staring out the front door at the heavy snow blanketing the street and the sidewalk. He knew he should go out and shovel off the sidewalk, but he wasn't feeling up to it. He'd let Soapy do it.

Petey's thoughts returned to the game and the things he'd heard Baxter tell his players. He thought about that for a long time and then glanced down at the sports page he'd been reading. His spirits hit rock bottom.

Even Joe Kennedy and Pete Williams, somewhat embarrassed, admitted that the high-scoring, fast action, run-and-gun basketball bubble had burst. Baxter's kind of basketball was fine for exhibitions and pickup games, but it clearly wasn't championship basketball. However, both writers agreed the experience had been entertaining for Valley Falls's hoop-crazy fans, and the Cancer Fund had benefited enormously.

Chip slept late Sunday morning. He came downstairs to find Biggie, Speed, Taps, and Red in the family room laughing and joking with his mom. It was just like old times.

Baxter made only a brief appearance, stopping for a moment on his way out for his morning stroll, before settling down to putting the finishing touches on his book.

A little later Petey showed up, announcing Soapy was extremely lonesome at the Sugar Bowl and had even promised to treat everyone to a "Soapy Delight" if they'd only come down and keep him company. Then Petey pulled Chip into the kitchen to tell him "something important!"

Petey told Chip what he'd heard at the game. "Chip, that Baxter guy's no good! He told his guys to foul you every time you got the ball. Called you a showboat and said if they fouled you a few times, you'd lose your cool and the officials would throw you out of the game! When he sent Mike into the game, he told him to play Barnes rough and talk trash to him because he couldn't take it! He said a lot of other things that made me realize what a fool I've been. He isn't a coach at all!

"And, Chip, I don't know if I should tell you this or not, but I got a letter from State, and they said Baxter never played anything but freshman ball. If that's true, he probably didn't even know your dad. What a liar!"

Petey was extremely bitter, but Chip made him promise not to tell anyone about the letter. Later that evening in the lab, Chip wrote two letters—one to the Gately Pottery Company and one to the University Alumni Association. He wrote that he was very anxious to locate Mr. T. A. K. Baxter, who'd graduated from State University about twenty-three or twenty-four years ago. It was extremely important.

Chip sat in the lab a long time thinking about Baxter and what Petey had said. Then he began to piece together some other things. First there was the water running from the tap in the sink. That was one of the things Chip never overlooked! He always shut the water off tight. He never forgot. And what about the cigarette ashes on the floor? And Mrs. Browning's remark about seeing Mr. Baxter coming up out of the basement several times? And the photo that didn't look like Baxter? And the piece of pottery that had been rough and unlike the others one day and identical with them the next time he looked at it? What was going on?

Why hadn't Baxter paid Petey Jackson? And if the man was such a big deal, why didn't he have nicer clothes and more luggage?

Chip's mom called him. First he made sure the water was shut off and the file locked, then he tucked the letters carefully in his pocket and joined his mom in the kitchen.

Valley Falls got back to normal during the next three days. The town's hoop fans seemed to realize once more that the Big Reds were still state champions and still in the race for Section Two honors. Pete Williams and Joe Kennedy did a thorough job of getting back on the Big Reds' bandwagon. The Independents and Baxter were barely mentioned.

Baxter had taken the defeat hard. It hadn't affected his campaign to snare J. P. Ohlsen, of course, but it did shake his confidence. The loss of the game was an unexpected blow to his pride. He resolved to work faster so he could get out of Valley Falls before things got too hot. He'd learned through experience that the "hit and run" was his best play, and he decided he'd have to pull off his deal as soon as possible. Of course, it didn't pay to rush a man like J. P. Ohlsen too fast. He had to play it smart. One little mistake in timing and the whole plan could blow up in his face. But time was running out!

CHAPTER 21

Basketball, Berrien, and Baxter

STEELTOWN AND Valley Falls were bitter sports rivals. Year in and year out these two teams were usually at the top, fighting for Section Two honors in all the major sports. This year the Iron Men were rugged, but the game was played in Valley Falls and the rebound from the three previous defeats was still strong enough to give Valley Falls the edge.

Rockwell started Browning at center, Hilton and Schwartz at the forwards, and Morris and Barnes at the guards. They played the whole game. It was a bitter, hard-fought, give-and-take contest, but the Big Reds ended up on the high end of the 56-53 score. Chip was high scorer with twenty-three points, and Brevin Barnes was next with eleven.

That victory gave the Big Reds the lift they needed, but then they ran into Northville on Friday. Rockwell had scouted Northville the Saturday after the Parkton loss and had prepared the Big Reds for Northville's possession game. The team wasn't surprised when the Northerners immediately went into their "deep freeze."

It was tantalizing basketball. Some coaches refer to this style of play as possession or percentage basketball. It is based on keeping the ball until an opponent makes a mistake and a wide-open shot is possible.

Rockwell had cautioned the Big Reds not to become anxious, not to make the mistake of lunging at the ball or trying for the interception. "That's what they want you to do," he warned. "So wait! Wait for them to make the first move. Remember, now, their whole style of play is based on the principle that their opponents can't score as long as they have the ball. They want a low-scoring game. And they'll only try a shot when you're faked out of position."

So Chip, Speed, Taps, Brevin, and Red waited. They waited through the first half and through the third quarter. Whenever the Northerners took a shot, the Big Reds jammed up the center and came out with the ball. They brought the ball slowly up the court and cautiously passed and passed until they had a good shot. Then they retreated and waited—waited until they thought they just couldn't wait any longer. But they did, smiling and talking to their opponents and holding back the urge to dive for a pass, just once.

The game was close. Northville would score and then the Big Reds would score, and the matching of baskets kept the Northerners in front by a single point. But time was running out. Now, with less than two minutes to go, Northville was content to run down the clock, holding the ball and continuing their deep-freeze attack.

Speed, watching the clock, decided to try his favorite play. Chip knew what was coming and got ready to cover Speed's man if the try was unsuccessful. Speed had played his opponent cautiously for thirty minutes. Now he played "dummy" perfectly, moving slowly, giving no hint he was going for the ball. Then, just as Chip's man passed across court to Speed's man, the Valley Falls speedster flashed forward. His extended fingers barely grazed the ball, but it was enough. The deflected ball eluded the panic-stricken grasp of Speed's man, and before he could recover, Speed hauled in the ball and dribbled furiously for the basket.

Two Northerners took out in hot pursuit, and Chip raced after them. It was a good thing he did. The taller player miraculously blocked Speed's shot. The ball careened off the backboard and directly above Chip's head. Chip's desperate leap carried his right hand above the rim and he jabbed frantically at the twirling ball. It was a lucky jab. The ball bobbed back up on the rim, hung there for an instant, and then fell through the net to put the Big Reds in the lead by a point.

Crowd hysteria gripped the Northerners then, and all the poise and assurance they'd shown controlling the ball for thirty-one minutes and twenty seconds vanished. A wild three-pointer was short and to the left of the basket, and Taps pulled the precious ball down, clutching it to his chest. Valley Falls had managed to defrost Northville's deep freeze and win by a score of 44-42.

Baxter didn't see the Big Reds win their thrilling game, but he heard Stan Gomez's broadcast on WTKO. He listened to the game sitting in the Ohlsen library following dinner.

Baxter enjoyed the evening immensely, using his suave, smooth speech to enthrall his listeners with stories of his worldly adventures searching for valuable clay deposits. Mrs. Ohlsen was visibly impressed, but Baxter was not too sure about J. P.'s reaction. However, he was more than pleased with his progress when Ohlsen invited him to tour the plant and have lunch with him the following Wednesday.

One of Baxter's special strategies employed to impress women such as Mary Hilton, Priscilla Ohlsen, and Karen Browning was to feign interest in their children. He'd made sure to learn all he could about the Ohlsens' only son. As the evening moved along and the basketball game brought Chip Hilton and the other Big Reds into the conversation, he cleverly maneuvered the parents into a discussion of their son, Joel.

Yes, Joel was their only son and a senior cadet at Manton Military Academy. He'd be home from February 26 until March 5, and they were eagerly anticipating his visit. J. P. planned to complete an important business trip early so he could be with his son during Joel's holiday.

Baxter made a mental note of the dates. It was obvious this man and woman idolized their son. If he couldn't finish the deal before Ohlsen left on his trip, the time when Joel would be home should be ideal. Ohlsen would be happy, receptive, and pliable.

The following Wednesday, before Ohlsen went away, Baxter tried to close his deal, but J. P. was in too much of a rush, and Baxter reluctantly withheld his proposition. He did lay the groundwork by taking Ohlsen into his confidence. He hinted he'd found a method for making pottery so exquisite it couldn't be distinguished from the revered Chelsea-Derby ware. The formula for that precious pottery had been lost long ago, but Baxter told J. P. he'd spent twenty years in developing a formula that, if it wasn't the original, produced ware that was just as good.

"Mr. Ohlsen, I have developed a formula of just the right mixture of hard paste and bone ash!"

Baxter proceeded to discuss soapstone, feldspar, kaolin, underglazes, overglazes, and soft pastes until he was holding Ohlsen in the palm of his hand. By this time, it was all he could do to control himself, but he was slick and knew from experience that delicate schemes such as this one often crashed and burned because of haste and poor timing. He reluctantly restrained his eagerness.

Just before leaving and wishing Ohlsen a successful trip, Baxter opened his briefcase and removed a thick file. He held it in his hand a moment, assuming a worried expression as if he wasn't sure he was doing the right thing. Then, abruptly, he laid the file on Ohlsen's desk.

"Mr. Ohlsen," he lowered his voice, "right there on your desk are several formulas that will produce the same ware the British potters produced a hundred years ago. This file contains test results, statistical analyses, and reports. They aren't complete, naturally. I have to protect nearly a lifetime's work, you know. But there's enough information there to convince any chemist of their possibilities.

"It doesn't cost any more to make the old Wedgwood, Delft, Copenhagen, or Spode than it does to make the ware they're creating in England today. These formulas right here . . . well, I think you'll find they speak for themselves, sir."

Baxter carefully studied the tall, distinguished man sitting behind the desk. "I'm leaving for Europe within the next two or three weeks. I'll be away for two or three years, and I'd like to see these formulas and certain other ceramic discoveries I have in good American hands.

"Perhaps you're the man who should be entrusted with them. I won't be able to devote any time to these formulas for several years, but I'd like to see the ware on its way. Suppose you look them over, and when you come back, I'll show you several pieces I roughed up from those formulas. You may get the surprise of your life!

"I guess this sounds foolish, but I wish you'd keep the file locked in your own safe and restricted to your own hands."

Ohlsen stared at the file this stranger had entrusted to his care. Here might be the answer he and hundreds of potters had been dreaming about. If the formulas worked, the Ohlsen pottery would have the means to make the finest china in the world right here at Valley Falls. Chelsea-Derby! Wedgwood! Majolica!

Ohlsen shook hands automatically with Baxter, almost in a daze as he watched the stranger leave his office. Then he reached for the file Baxter had left on his desk.

As Baxter expected, his plans made little progress during the next two weeks while Ohlsen was away, but the Big Reds had made decided progress since their clash with Steeltown. After the Northville game, they met Hampton at home on Friday, February 7, and won by a score of 59-41.

On the following Friday, captain Bill Berrien and his Southerners came to town. The Southern contest was a "must" game for the Big Reds. Southern had only one loss and was leading Section Two. Valley Falls had been defeated three times. One more defeat meant they'd be out of the running. Besides, they had a score to settle with this team that had trounced the Big Reds on that never-to-be-forgotten night of January 10. They were more keyed-up for the Southern game than they'd been for the Independents.

Berrien lined up against Hilton again, but he couldn't stop the big, blond forward this time. Chip was getting the ball now and was too clever for the rugged Southern battler. Chip finished with twenty-two points to Berrien's seven. Speed and Brevin brought the ball up the floor with dazzling alacrity and passed to Chip, Taps, and Red. The Southerners fought gamely, but they couldn't cope with the fierce team fight of the Big Reds. That was the difference. Valley Falls won, 56-48.

Berrien left the game with half a minute to go, and he and Chip exchanged friendly handshakes. As Chip walked with him to the Southern bench, Berrien received a standing ovation. The Valley Falls fans were celebrating his leadership and moral authority in the crucial stand he'd taken at Southern. Brevin was so proud he could hardly speak as he dashed to the Southern bench and raised Berrien's arm aloft.

Meanwhile, Baxter was spending the most anxious two weeks of his life waiting for J. P. Ohlsen's return. He was stressed and worried. Was something going to ruin all his careful planning?

One morning he was badly jolted. He'd slept late and had come downstairs just as the mail arrived. He waited until the postal carrier was out of sight and then opened the door, fishing the letters out of the mailbox.

Baxter inspected each letter casually. Most of the mail was for Mary Hilton, but there were two letters for Chip. The first one was postmarked "University" and he tossed it down on the coffee table. Then he noticed the return address of the other envelope—the Gately Pottery Company, Columbus, Ohio.

Baxter's body stiffened as he inspected the envelope carefully. He thrust it in his pocket and started up to his room. At the landing, he paused. He had a hunch . . . It wouldn't do any harm to take the letter from the university too.

BASKETBALL, BERRIEN, AND BAXTER

In his room, he tore the envelopes open and his worst fears were realized. The Gately letter was from the personnel department. Baxter read the words half aloud: "No person by the name of T. A. K. Baxter has ever been employed by this company."

Baxter muttered an oath and tore open the university letter. He cursed again as he read: "We regret to advise you that T. A. K. Baxter, an alumnus of State University, to whom you referred in your letter of January 27, is deceased. Mr. Baxter was prominent in the field of chemistry and was living at his home in Padget, Indiana, at the time of his death."

Baxter had read enough. So the kid was suspicious. There was no time to lose. He'd have to close in on Ohlsen as soon as he returned. In the meantime, he'd have to watch the mail every day. He'd known the kid was smart . . .

CHAPTER 22

Jenkins Shows His True Colors

HOOP FEVER gripped Valley Falls again after the Steeltown game on February 21. The Big Reds played their best game of the year, winning 63-62, capitalizing on Chip's scoring spree of thirty-two points. Now everyone was talking tournament. It was too late to win the championship of Section Two because Southern had completed its schedule with just two losses. But there was a chance from the runner-up spot to duplicate last year's winning of the state championship tournament.

Valley Falls was excited over the Big Reds' comeback. Delford and Valley Falls were running neck and neck, each with three defeats. The two tied teams would clash on the Delford court on February 28, the last game of the season. The Big Reds were sure they could take Delford.

Every day Chip had expected replies from the university and the Gately Pottery Company, but each day he'd been disappointed. Three weeks had gone by since he'd mailed those letters. Could the replies be lost in the mail? Surely not both of them! Maybe the letters had come when his mom was at work and he was at school . . . when only Baxter was there.

Perhaps Baxter had intercepted them! Chip sat down and wrote again—this time enclosing stamped envelopes addressed to him at the Sugar Bowl.

The next few days were long and tiresome for everyone but T. A. K. Baxter. Baxter was putting the pressure on Ohlsen, who'd returned on Monday. He and Baxter had been closeted together in the pottery office every morning and afternoon since.

The Big Reds found practice tedious. Rockwell was irritable, and the town hoop fans were anxious. Wednesday night, Chip was in the storeroom trying to study when he heard a shout and laughter. A moment later, the door opened and a tall young man dressed in a dark gray military uniform blocked the light. At first Chip scarcely knew him. But then he recognized Joel Ohlsen. What a difference!

"Fats," Chip cried, rushing forward. Then he stopped. "I'm sorry, Joel—"

Ohlsen grinned. "Forget it," he said, extending his hand. "Don't apologize for the 'Fats.' I *was* fat. Now that I've lost forty pounds, I don't mind it at all. Used to make me real mad, though. But then, I wasn't very nice to you either, was I? How've you been, Chipper?"

"Busy as always. It's great to see you, Joel!"

Joel Ohlsen smiled. "It's good to see you too, Chip," he said with great sincerity. "I want you to know you're the first person I've looked up since I came home. How 'bout I stop over tomorrow night? It'll be like the old days. I'd like to see your mom too. How about 7:30?"

"Great, Joel, it'll be like old times," Chip said. "Mom'll be glad to see you."

Joel flecked an imaginary speck of dust off his coat sleeve and then grinned. "How do you like the uniform? I'll wear the real dressy one tomorrow night, just for your mom. See ya later!"

Joel Ohlsen, wearing his best uniform, arrived at the Hiltons' just as Baxter was leaving. They exchanged quick glances and a nod, but neither spoke. Mary Hilton hugged Joel. It was like old times!

Joel asked Chip about Baxter. "He lives here?"

Chip was surprised. "You know him?" he asked. "Yes, he stays here. Says he played ball with Dad at State."

"I don't know him," Joel said slowly, studying Chip, "but Dad knows him. You don't like him!" he said flatly.

Chip admitted he wasn't particularly fond of Baxter, but added nothing else.

"I don't like his looks either," Joel responded, "and I'd like to know what he and Dad have going. Baxter came to the office yesterday with five or six pieces of pottery, and they played with them all afternoon."

Chip was startled but quickly changed the subject. As soon as Joel left, he hurried down to the lab. His hands shook as he unlocked the door and hurried to the table where he'd placed the five pieces of pottery. He examined each piece carefully. This wasn't his father's work! Now all the pieces felt like that one odd piece had felt. They were imitations!

He sat down by the file and tried to figure it out. If this wasn't his dad's pottery, then someone had been in the lab and switched these copies for the originals. How? The lab door was always locked.

It had to be Baxter! Mrs. Browning had seen him coming out of the basement. Also, Baxter smoked. That would account for the ashes. The running water was proof someone had been there. The five original pieces were gone, and five imitations had taken their place. Why? Joel said Baxter had five or six pieces of pottery at J. P.'s office.

Chip snapped his fingers. That was it! He'd go see Mr. Ohlsen. Better yet, he'd take the imitations with him. Was Baxter planning some kind of joke on him? After all, how had Baxter—or whoever it was—gotten into the lab? The door hadn't been damaged. He knew he hadn't left it unlocked.

Chip was so busy studying, working at the Sugar Bowl, and preparing for the game at Delford that he didn't have time to think much more about Baxter the rest of the evening. That night one of the worst snowstorms in years gripped Valley Falls. The next day buses ran late and driving was difficult. School was a farce. Noisy, excited students arrived late, cold and wet from snowball fights. But storm or no storm, every student had one thought in mind—that night's game at Delford.

Rockwell took one look at the accumulating snow and immediately canceled the bus. Just before the 11:00 class change, Mr. Zimmerman announced that the interstate between Valley Falls and Delford was closed because a truck had overturned, spilling its contents. The basketball squad would take the train to Delford instead of the bus. The train was slower but the only way to get there. And no one wanted to cancel a Delford game! The traveling squad was to assemble in the gym at noon.

Speed, sitting in A. P. history class, turned and shook his head. Chip knew exactly what he meant. The train to Delford took three hours. With the weather and the transfer at Valley Junction, it would be an uncomfortable trip. And uncomfortable it was! The train they were supposed to take at 1:00 was late. They arrived at Valley Junction at 2:30 instead of 2:00, missing their connection to Delford. An hour later, Rogers managed to get seats on the only thing headed to Delford. The engine pulled several freight cars and one antiquated coach.

The storm grew worse as they chugged north. At 5:00 it was snowing so hard no one could see out the windows. But that wasn't the worst of it. The passenger coach, with its old red seats, was stone-cold—and it got colder as the heating system weakened. Besides the Valley Falls group and Stan Gomez of WTKO, there were only a dozen or so passengers on the train. Mothers with their small children complained bitterly to the conductor and his crew, but there was nothing they could do.

Soapy tried to lighten the mood by pointing to a hole in one of the windows. "We're experiencing history! This coach was last used way back in 1861. Look, here's where one of the Rebels' bullets hit!"

But Soapy's effort fell flat, and soon the coach was quiet except for crying children. The snow was piling up on the track. The train made stop after stop. Each time it was harder to get under way again. Finally, nearly two miles from Delford, their destination, it stopped for good.

The conductor announced that the plow they'd been following had broken down and they'd have to wait until it was repaired. Rockwell asked how long he thought that would take, and he replied, "One guess is as good as another, but I figure at least two hours."

"Two hours!" Rockwell repeated, turning to Prof Rogers. "That's no good! It's 6:00 now! What'll we do, Prof?"

Rogers cast a worried glance at the boys. Each one was huddled up in his seat, crowding as close as possible to his seatmate. Chip and the other players had covered the small children with their varsity jackets.

"Maybe we ought to hike it, Hank. The boys look half frozen," Rogers chattered.

Rockwell asked the conductor if there was a road nearby. The conductor shook his head emphatically. "I wouldn't try it," he said. "It's a mile away and I doubt if the road crew has plowed. If you're going to walk, you'd be better off following the track."

The other passengers decided they might as well freeze trying to get somewhere as freeze sitting still. Bundled up, they piled out and strung out in a long line to plod through the deep snow, heads bent against the stinging blizzard. There was some banter in the beginning, but as they found it increasingly difficult to breathe in the face of the biting wind, they soon became silent, taking turns breaking the path.

Chip, Speed, Soapy, and Red each carried one of the small kids. It was rough going, and although the others helped with the young bundles, they were fighting for every step and every breath.

It was 7:30 when the shivering Valley Falls basketball team ringed the fireplace in the hotel. They were so exhausted they could hardly move. Chip wanted only one thing, a warm bed—and lots of time to spend in it.

"Get the kids to their rooms right away, Chet," Rockwell ordered. "I'll call Jenkins and see if we can postpone the game until tomorrow."

Stewart and Rogers exchanged glances. They knew Rock would rather walk back to Valley Falls in the blizzard than ask Jenkins for a favor.

"When that blinkin' rat, as Soapy calls him, hears the shape we're in after battling through the snow," Chet observed bitterly, "you can be sure he'll insist on playing tonight!"

Chet was right. Jenkins wouldn't postpone. He said

the officials were already at the high school, the crowd was growing, and Valley Falls wasn't the only place where it snowed.

How about his team? They'd been battling the snow too. Furthermore, just because Rockwell and his wimps had won the state championship last year, they had no right to try to run all the basketball schedules in the state. His team would be ready to play at 8:30, and he'd demand that the officials forfeit the game to Delford if Rockwell and his delicate little team didn't show up.

When Chip and the team heard that, they were pumped! If that was the way Delford wanted it, so be it! The Big Reds weren't pulling out of any game as long as they could stand on their feet.

The game was played. Only a sprinkling of spectators were in the stands, and Rockwell chalked up another mark in his long score against Jinx Jenkins for that lie. The officials were there, all right, and agreed that according to the letter of the rules, Jenkins was right about the forfeiture.

The game was sheer torture. Each team was geared up. The Big Reds were full of fight, but they were so tired they could scarcely move. Chip's arms and legs were weak, not from the cold but with a numbing fatigue. Taps got a cramp and had to be helped off the court, writhing in pain. Red and Brevin managed to play a pretty good first half, but in the second half, they faded with every minute. If it hadn't been for Chip, Speed, and Soapy, the game would have been a complete blowout.

Chip and Speed played their hearts out. Red Henry and his teammates played hard. This game meant an invitation to the state tournament. They played to win but sympathized with the plight of their opponents. Strangely enough, the sparse Delford crowd cheered for the Valley Falls team more than they did their own. The word had gotten around that Jenkins had forced these exhausted kids to play when they were hardly able to stand up, and the fans, what few there were, booed Jenkins every time he made a move. That was small consolation for a group of sick, tired, and broken-spirited kids who were playing on sheer nerve. Only Chip's fighting leadership and Speed's and Soapy's burning desire kept the Big Reds in the game. It even looked for a while as though desire and leadership were going to triumph.

Delford led at the half, 24-18. In the second half, Chip took charge of the scoring and picked up twenty points practically by himself. He was hot, and the rest of the Big Reds, following Rockwell's instructions, gave him the ball every time they came down the court. With ten seconds to play, the Big Reds scored and were in front, 47-46.

Standing out of bounds, Red Henry fired the ball to his teammate at midcourt. Only Speed's quick reflexes deflected the ball out of bounds, preventing a sure unguarded drive to the basket. The ball ricocheted off the corner of the scorer's table and into the stands. Chip, Speed, Soapy, Bill English, and Red Schwartz were giving their last ounce of energy to hold on to that slim one-point lead. Then it happened!

Five seconds to play! Taking the inbounds pass, a Delford guard heaved a desperation shot. Every player, coach, official, and spectator followed the flight of the ball, and every eye gauged its trajectory. It was going to sail over the backboard! The Delford players groaned. Then the crowd uttered an elongated gasp of astonishment as the ball seemed almost to stop in flight before dropping like a rock.

The exultant shout that had erupted from the Big Reds changed to dismay as they saw the ball falling toward the ring as though it had eyes! Down the ball fell, and then it thudded to rest, in fact seemed to droop, over the six-inch arm that separates the ring from the backboard.

Ten players stood motionless, mouths agape, staring at the ball coming to rest momentarily on the very edge of the basket. While they looked on in amazement, they heard the air whooshing out as the deflating ball slumped through the basket.

Chip flashed an agonized look at the referee holding both arms over his head, and Chip's dismayed eyes watched the scoreboard blink three times and then register Delford 49, Valley Falls 47.

The place went wild! Rockwell was on the floor arguing with the officials. Jinx Jenkins, waving the rule book, shouted at the top of his voice that the basket counted. After a long argument and repeated reference to the rule book, Rockwell was finally convinced that the officials and Jenkins were right. That was the way it had to be. "Could only happen in Delford," Rock grumbled to himself, shaking his head. "A blizzard, a buffoon, and a deflating ball!" It was the final straw in a day and an evening of mishaps, disappointments, and heartbreaks for the Big Reds.

CHAPTER 23

Hometown Rally

MARY HILTON and her colleagues had their hands full at the phone company the next morning with another storm. But this storm was personal, brought about partly because the Big Reds had lost at Delford but primarily because of the spellbinding wizardry of Valley Falls's own WTKO sports expert, Stan Gomez.

Gomez, on the trip to Delford, had witnessed Big Red fellowship in action. He'd seen the players give their varsity jackets to the women and children and then sit shivering through the long, cold ride from Valley Junction. Then he'd stumbled and slipped and waded and fought his way through the heavy snow and the bitter winter night, marveling at the gallantry of the team in the straggling line up ahead as they struggled through the snow, breaking a path and carrying the youngsters piggyback. He watched the teenagers unselfishly help those who needed help so badly.

Later, Gomez had caught the significance of Jenkins's refusal to postpone so he could play a weakened team or make Valley Falls forfeit. He called it a dirty trick. Gomez also hadn't forgotten the reaction of the Delford players to the extremes to which their coach would go to win. Gomez also had caught something more. He'd caught the repugnance of the hoop-crazed Delford fans to Jenkins's poor sportsmanship.

The way Gomez felt about everything he'd observed and heard was sufficient to fire him with a fervor of speech that came from the heart, thrilling every man, woman, and child listening to his broadcast. Just about everyone in Valley Falls was listening that bitter winter evening, and just about everyone in Delford not at the game was listening too. Never before did a sports announcer have such a sympathetic audience. Before the game was over, thousands of fireside listeners knew they'd been hearing not only a stirring account of a nerve-tingling basketball game but one of the most dramatic stories of unconscious heroism that had ever been told on the air.

The Delford community wasted no time doing something about the way they felt. They got busy on their telephones that night and early the next morning. Their insistence led to an emergency meeting of the Delford board of education and the prompt dismissal of Jinx Jenkins, a man who should never have been in charge of kids. Letters were sent to Carl L. Zimmerman, principal of Valley Falls High School, and the state athletic association detailing their regret over Jinx Jenkins's handling of the circumstances, announcing his dismissal, and expressing their desire to replay the game.

So sincere and so inspiring were Stan Gomez's words that everyone in Valley Falls forgot all about the outcome of the game and the end of their tournament hopes. They remembered only that their kids, who wore their Valley Falls colors, did the right thing in extending their hands unselfishly and courageously even though it meant the loss of their chance at the state championship.

Rockwell, Rogers, Stewart, Chip, and his teammates knew nothing about all this. Coming back on the train the next day, they were steeped in despair and defeat— sick in body, some of them, and sick at heart, all of them.

At the junction, some of the players bought papers, and Chip caught a glimpse of the sports page headline. It was something about Southern and Delford. Too tired to care much about it, he dozed off again. Taps and Brevin were both running a fever and anxious to get home.

As the train neared Valley Falls, Chip began to think how difficult it was going to be facing their fans. He looked out the window and couldn't help thinking how tough it was going to be tonight at the Sugar Bowl, and he wished he didn't have to work. Then he began to think about Baxter, but somehow or other he didn't seem to care what the man was up to. He was just too tired to care about anything right now. Finally he closed his eyes again and tried to rest.

The train passed Morrisville, the brickyard, and the pottery and started slowing down for Valley Falls. Chip thought he heard the sound of music. He thought, at first, someone must have a radio on the train, but then the music began to register: it was the Valley Falls Victory March! Chip shook his head and felt sure he was imagining things. The music grew stronger and, like everyone else, he peered out the window to see where the music was coming from on this gray winter day.

He saw the entire band in their Valley Falls red-and-white capes, playing the Victory March! Dink Davis and his squad were yelling and waving banners. The whole platform was jammed with cheering kids and men and women. Chip couldn't figure out what was going on.

The train stopped with a lurch and the hissing of air brakes. Rockwell led the way through the aisle and down the steps with his shoulders squared and his chin up, and the team followed.

You'd have thought the president of the United States had arrived in Valley Falls! Chip had never heard such cheering! He and his teammates were hustled through the crowd that surged closer and closer until they came to a small, portable stage. Principal Zimmerman stood there, smiling and applauding like everyone else. Chip still didn't know what it was all about. The Big Reds were pushed up on the stage.

Zimmerman was beginning to speak. As though from a great distance, Chip heard him telling Rock and the team how proud Valley Falls was of their service, sportsmanship, and determination and the way they'd acted and played at Delford. Chip didn't hear it all, but he heard enough to realize that though the people of Valley Falls were hoop crazy, they weren't quitters—they didn't quit on their kids and their coach just because of a score in a game. They knew what was important!

As Zimmerman talked and the crowd cheered, the bitterness and tightness in Chip's throat and the heartache and hurt feeling that had swelled his chest were gone. Chip looked at the guys. Their eyes were bright now, and some were smiling. Rockwell's mouth was slanted into that crooked smile. All the despair of the Big Reds suddenly seemed to have vanished. It was as though a storm that had been raging suddenly quieted and left nothing behind but clean streets and a new, clear, sunny day.

It wasn't so bad that afternoon at the Sugar Bowl, after all. Petey, John Schroeder, and Doc Jones were cheerful, saying they'd had their share of championships and to "wait until next year!"

Later, Petey dropped two letters on the storeroom desk, one at a time. "There's your scholarship from State, Chipper," he said, grinning cheerfully, "and here's a letter from a pottery company. Probably want the formula for that pottery you sold at the exhibit."

Chip's heart jumped.

He thanked Petey, tossing the letters carelessly on the desk. But as soon as Petey left, he tore them open. The first letter, from State, was a copy of their original letter. They were sorry it hadn't arrived. "We regret to advise you that T. A. K. Baxter, an alumnus of State University, to whom you referred in your letter of January 27, is deceased. He . . . ."

The second was from the Gately Pottery Company, and it, too, said this was a copy of their original letter. "No person by the name of T. A. K. Baxter is employed by this company!"

Chip sat there a long time studying the letters, mulling over their significance again and again. Baxter was a fake. Assuming someone else's identity. Had lied about being an executive in the Gately Company. Anyway, that settled it! Tomorrow he'd see J. P. Ohlsen and tell him the whole story.

Chip was dead tired after a busy Saturday night at the Sugar Bowl, but he couldn't get to sleep. He hadn't seen the impostor since he'd been home, but his mom said Mr. Baxter had been working awfully hard at the pottery with Mr. Ohlsen.

"He's been at the pottery every night, Chip. He's there tonight! His book is finished and he leaves for England next week."

Baxter was up early the next morning and out of the house before Chip came downstairs. After breakfast, Chip read the papers. The sports pages were chiefly concerned with the Delford game and the letter from the Delford principal offering to replay the game. Chip read again what Joe Kennedy and Pete Williams had written in Saturday's papers: "Valley Falls High School appreciated the spirit and sportsmanship that prompted the offer to replay the game. All concerned agreed, a game once played and lost couldn't be re-won. As far as the Big Reds, Coach Rockwell, the students, and the Valley Falls basketball fans were concerned, Delford had earned the right to their invitation to the tournament."

Chip was dreading the information he was going to share with J. P. Ohlsen. He decided he couldn't put it off any longer. As he neared the house on the hill, he remembered a previous visit to this home. He always seemed to be in a jam when he called on his father's old boss.

Joel beat the butler to open the door. He'd been in the library and had seen Chip walking up the long drive.

"Hi ya, Chipper. What you doin' up here this time of day?"

"I wanted to see your father for a couple of minutes."

"He's not home, Chip. He's at the office. Important?"

Chip nodded. "It's important to me, Joel. I've got to see him today!"

Joel smiled. "That's easy! Wait till I get my car and I'll drive you."

Chip started to protest but Joel stopped him. "No big deal. That's what friends are for. Come on! I'll drop you by the gate. You don't mind if I rush back? Got to take Mom someplace."

After Joel dropped him at the pottery gate, Chip tried the main door but it was locked. He then walked to the side entrance where the Sunday watchman, Sam McQueen, was on duty.

McQueen knew Chip and grinned. "Where do you think you're going, young man?"

"Hi, Mr. McQueen. I'd like to see Mr. Ohlsen, if he's not too busy."

"Well, he's busy, all right! Fact is, he's so busy he left strict orders no one was to be admitted. Got DeWitt up there and a guy named Baxter. Been up there all day. Doesn't want to be disturbed! Even told me not to come up and check the office!"

"But I've got to see him," Chip insisted.

McQueen shook his head decisively. "Sorry, Chip, I can't let you in. If it's that important, you can wait by the door. He can't stay in there forever.

"Well," McQueen smiled, "I hope you get to see him. Got to make rounds now. Sorry I couldn't let you in, Chipper."

Chip leaned against the stone wall by the office door and resigned himself to a long wait. And it was a long wait. The hours dragged. His feet were cold, and he kicked the toes of his shoes against the wall to keep the circulation going. He got hungry, and then the tired feeling that had gripped him during the past few days returned. Still he waited. Twice, McQueen, on his rounds, stopped to speak to Chip and went away shaking his head. At last, at 6:00, Marty DeWitt and T. A. K. Baxter came out of the building and walked briskly away through the evening dusk.

Chip had started when the door opened, but when he saw who it was, he stood quietly by the wall as DeWitt and Baxter passed by a few feet away. He thought Baxter's eyes flickered sideways in his direction, but he couldn't be sure.

As soon as they were out of sight, Chip knocked on the door and was rewarded, at last, when Ohlsen heard him.

"Hello, Chip. What are you doing here?"

"I'd like to talk to you about something important, Mr. Ohlsen."

"That's fine, Chip, but I'm awfully busy. If it isn't urgent, I'd rather talk to you tomorrow."

"But it is urgent, Mr. Ohlsen. It's about Mr. Baxter!"

"Baxter? What about Baxter? Here, come into my office. Sit down and tell me what's bothering you."

"Well, Mr. Ohlsen, maybe it's not as important as I think it is, but, I don't think Mr. Baxter is Mr. Baxter. I mean, well, here's a letter I got from the Gately Pottery Company where he claims he worked and here's another from the university, and they . . . Well, you can read them."

Ohlsen was alert now, and his hands trembled as he grasped the letters. As he read, he gradually pushed them further and further across the desk, as if he didn't want to believe the words. His eyes were disturbed and his face was worried.

"What prompted you to write to State and Gately, Chip?"

Chip told him about the photo that didn't resemble the stranger and about the basement lab. His suspicions about Baxter's integrity had grown after Petey received a letter from the university. Then he told how Baxter had acted on the bench in the Cancer Fund game and how that had bothered him, so he'd written the letters. Finally, Chip told Ohlsen about the peculiar changes in the five pieces of pottery.

Ohlsen bolted upright in his chair. When Chip finished, J. P. walked over to the safe, returned with a cardboard box, and took out five pieces of pottery.

"Are these the pieces?" Ohlsen asked, his voice tense.

"They sure look like them. If they're not Dad's, they're exact duplicates!"

"And you're sure there are five pieces of pottery in your lab right now?" Ohlsen demanded.

"Well, Mr. Ohlsen, they were there when I left this afternoon."

Ohlsen turned away from his desk and began to pace nervously back and forth across the office. His brow was wrinkled, and Chip could see he was deeply moved. He turned to Chip once more.

"Chip," he said searchingly, "are you sure these are the same size and shape as the ones in your Dad's lab? Are you positive?"

Chip nodded. "Yes, sir! Identical!"

J. P. was laboring under terrific emotion now. His voice was sharp and the words almost tumbled one over the other as he spoke. "Chip, I want you to go right home and bring me those pieces you have in your lab! And another thing—bring along a few of your father's formulas. And don't say a word to a soul about this, not even your mother. Hurry!"

CHAPTER 24

Baxter Fouls Out

WHEN BAXTER had stepped out of the pottery doorway, the quick glance Chip had caught was comprehensive even though cleverly concealed. DeWitt hadn't noticed Chip at all, but Baxter saw him, and his confidence suddenly shattered. This venture had been on the verge of success. In fact, he'd reeled in Ohlsen completely. But now something told him there was trouble ahead.

When DeWitt drove away, Baxter hastily retraced his steps. It was just about dark, and his footsteps were silent as he hurried from the snow-covered parking lot to the shadow of an old building. With anxious eyes, he watched the light in Ohlsen's office. Although he couldn't see Chip and didn't know whether he was in the office or not, he could see Ohlsen pacing. He didn't dare leave. He had to know whether or not that kid was in the office, and if he was, he had to know what he and Ohlsen were talking about.

A few minutes later, Chip emerged from the building and hurried away. Baxter followed at a safe distance, but when Chip started to jog along the slippery streets, he had difficulty keeping up. He was close enough, however, to see Chip enter his darkened house. He watched as the light flashed on in the basement a few seconds later. If only he could see what the kid was doing in the basement.

Chip was doing exactly what Baxter was afraid of, wrapping the five pieces of pottery in newspaper and placing them in a small box. Then he opened the filing cabinet and took out several bundles of his father's formulas before leaving the lab and going upstairs.

Outside, the biting wind in his face made Chip wish he had the car as he started back to the pottery.

Baxter saw the box and thought the worst. When he saw Chip jogging back toward the pottery, Baxter knew for certain his scheme was ruined. How did the kid find out?

The letters Baxter had intercepted had been the tip-off. The kid had been suspicious, and something must have happened to confirm his suspicions. What now? Run? How could he? Where could he go? He didn't have any money. Leave now with thousands of dollars almost in his grasp?

Then Baxter thought of the large brown envelope in Ohlsen's office safe, and he suddenly broke into a run. He had to pass that kid and beat him to the office.

He stopped in the shadows of the pottery entrance. While he waited, he fitted the heavy key case in his right hand and thumped his left several times. Baxter had always prided himself on his cleverness and ability to get out of difficult situations without using a lethal weapon. He pulled off his belt, rolled it up, and placed it in his coat pocket.

Chip came along the street, deep in thought about Baxter and this pottery mystery. He saw only a swiftly moving shadow and ducked instinctively—but not soon enough. Baxter's fist, reinforced by his key case, cracked him on the side of his face. The vicious blow staggered Chip and, even as he fell, Baxter struck him again. This time the blow landed at the back of his neck, and Chip fell heavily into the snow. The box he'd been carrying dropped, the contents spilling out onto the sidewalk.

Baxter dragged Chip quickly into the shadows. He pulled his belt out of his pocket and strapped Chip's hands behind his back. Making a gag out of his handkerchief, he callously tied it behind Chip's head. As hatred for this kid welled up in his heart, Baxter thumped Chip's head roughly against the snow-covered ground. He rolled Chip against the fence before hurrying toward Ohlsen's office.

The sudden change in events had left J. P. Ohlsen confused and disappointed. After Chip hurried out of the office, Ohlsen slumped down in his chair. He shook his head and tried to figure out how he'd allowed himself to be tricked and made the fall guy by such a cheap con man. He groaned as he remembered how he'd rushed to swallow this convincing stranger's bait—hook, line, and sinker. If word of this ever got out, he'd be the laughingstock of everyone in the industry.

While Ohlsen was sitting there berating himself, Baxter quietly opened the outside door and crept softly along the hall and up the stairs. When he reached Ohlsen's half-open office door, he paused. He had to make this good. His right hand was bunched menacingly in his coat pocket as he gently pushed the door open with his left hand and stepped into the office. Ohlsen was so deep in thought, he never even looked up.

"Come in, Chip. Put them on the desk."

Then he glanced up and saw Baxter standing in the door. Momentarily bewildered, J. P. rose angrily to his feet. "You—"

Baxter's pocketed hand jerked upward, and he ominously moved forward. "No, you, Ohlsen. You! Sit in that chair and keep your mouth shut, or I may have to close it!"

Baxter's eyes shifted toward the safe and back to Ohlsen. A smirk of satisfaction stole across his lips. "Good," he sneered, "the safe is still open! I was hoping I might not have to force you to give me the combination! Let's complete our business right now instead of waiting. I happen to be in more of a hurry than I'd planned."

Keeping his hand in his pocket, he moved quickly to Ohlsen's desk, swiftly tying J. P.'s arms behind the chair.

Ohlsen didn't move, but his eyes flashed with anger. "You'll never get away with this, Baxter," he promised through tight lips. "Never!"

Baxter's response was a brutal slap with the back of his hand against Ohlsen's mouth. "Shut up, Ohlsen!" he threatened. "When I call your house, tell your butler to send your car down here. Tell him to park it in front of the building and give me the keys and then to go on home because we'll probably be working all night. Got it? When that car gets here, you, me, and a nosy kid named Chip Hilton are going for a ride! No, not the kind of ride you're thinking of—not unless you try to get out of hand! We're men of the world. I imagine you won't to be too anxious to let people know what a fool the great J. P. Ohlsen turned out to be."

Baxter dialed the Ohlsen residence and held the phone to Ohlsen's mouth. Ohlsen ordered his car be brought to the office immediately and the keys given to Mr. Baxter at the front door.

Baxter smiled with satisfaction. "Very good, Mr. J. P. Ohlsen," he said smoothly, "very good! I'll have to have expense money, naturally, for my trip to England. Don't get up," he laughed. "I can help myself."

Baxter opened the safe door wider. He tossed papers and other contents carelessly on the floor. One small door inside the safe was locked, and Baxter smiled sarcastically as he pulled the packet of keys out of his pocket.

Gradually Chip's senses returned. He realized his hands were tied behind his back and his face was jammed deep down in the snow. His mind clicked back to the events that had just happened. It had to be Baxter who'd slugged him. Suddenly he remembered Mr. Ohlsen was waiting for him in the office.

He violently wrenched at the belt to get his hands free. When he finally got them loose, he struggled painfully to gain his feet. He got to one knee, then suddenly felt as though Baxter had struck him again. A sharp, piercing pain in the back of his head nearly dropped him into unconsciousness again. He grasped a handful of snow and held it to the back of his head.

Chip staggered once or twice and fell against the fence as he looked up and down the street. Then he caught sight of the lights in J. P.'s office and started in that direction, weaving a bit but gradually regaining his strength and his wits.

He was surprised to find the outside door unlocked. When he got inside, it was so quiet he was scared. Maybe something had happened to Mr. Ohlsen . . .

He slipped quietly up the steps and then heard a rustling noise. Through the open door he saw Baxter at the safe. Tiptoeing forward, he saw Mr. Ohlsen tied to the chair.

J. P. saw Chip at the same time and shook his head in warning, mouthing to Chip to go for help. But Chip kept moving toward Baxter. Baxter sensed a presence and swung around.

"Watch out, Chip," Ohlsen shouted, "He's got a gun!"

But Chip wasn't watching out for anything. He only knew that T. A. K. Baxter, or whoever he was, had caused him a lot of trouble and had slugged him. Now he appeared to be robbing J. P. Ohlsen's safe. Chip hurled himself across the room at Baxter's crouched figure. Ohlsen was horrified to see Baxter's hand come out of his pocket. But then Ohlsen was relieved to see that all Baxter held was a short piece of wood.

Chip didn't see anything except the smirking face of the man he despised and whom he now saw unmasked for the criminal he really was. Chip hadn't fully recovered, but he was fired by an intense fury that added to his strength. He smashed head on into Baxter in a clumsy body block and they went down in a heap, struggling desperately as they thrashed around on the floor.

Ohlsen shouted for help and struggled so hard to free himself that he and the chair tumbled to the floor. There they were, all three wrestling and straining and battling on the office rug when Sam McQueen dashed breathlessly into the room.

Before McQueen could grasp the situation, Baxter was up on his feet and rushing for the door. Chip launched himself in one desperate flying tackle at Baxter's heels, and the two tall figures crashed into McQueen and then he was on the floor, too. All he accomplished was to catch one of Baxter's weakened blows on the right ear.

Chip was in control now. McQueen heard Ohlsen shouting that one Sam McQueen would be out of a job if he didn't untie his hands right away. So Sam crawled over the spilled chair and loosened Ohlsen's hands. Then he crawled over to help Chip hold a silenced con man on the floor while Ohlsen called the police.

After the police had taken Baxter away, Ohlsen leaned back in his chair and held his head. On the other side of the desk, Chip Hilton leaned forward and held his head. The mirrored expressions prompted each to a grin, sickly as it was. Ohlsen then got up and went to the safe.

He came back, holding a large brown envelope and told Chip to open it. Chip opened the envelope and saw more money than he'd ever seen in his life.

Ohlsen watched the surprised expression on Chip's face and smiled at his astonishment. "Yes, Chip, fifty thousand dollars, and he'd have had it all the first thing in the morning if it hadn't been for you.

"You see, Chip," Ohlsen continued, "Marty DeWitt and I both fell for his formulas because the ware on the desk—your father's ware—is wonderful work. But it's the clay content of those pieces that sold me. Of course, I didn't know that until tonight. I thought it was the formula that was responsible for the beautiful work.

"Today we can't get that kind of clay in quantity. Baxter counted on that. He was clever enough to know that the clay and not the formulas was responsible for the ware. So, he substituted the imitation pieces and brought the real pieces here as his specimens.

"Baxter wanted to sell the formulas for cash now and then royalty payments upon production. Said we couldn't arrange a wire deposit since he'd closed all his bank accounts and wanted to use the cash to invest in overseas markets.

"Everything was all set for tomorrow. He was to deliver the complete formulas to my office at 8:00, sign the receipt for the money you have there, and then catch his flight to Europe.

"You saved the pottery fifty thousand dollars and saved me embarrassment in front of the entire industry. I sincerely appreciate all you've done for me and the pottery! And I regret that Baxter used your father's research and experiments."

Ohlsen counted out fifty one-hundred-dollar bills and placed them in Chip's hands. "I'd be honored, son, if you'd add this to your college fund."

"I couldn't, Mr. Ohlsen—I didn't do anything! Mom wouldn't stand for it! Besides, I'm glad I got to see the great T. A. K. Baxter get what he deserved!"

Ohlsen's smile was understanding as he took the money from Chip's outstretched hands.

"All right, Chipper," he said gently, "I'll talk to your mother about it tomorrow. She and I understand each other. There are several ways of adding to a great kid's college fund. Now, I'll have my car take you home, and you have Mary Hilton put a cold compress on that head of yours. You're going to need it when you get to State!"

• • •

THE SPRING OF Chip Hilton's senior year at Valley Falls High is probably the most exciting time of his high school career. A pebble, the "House That Rock Built," and dramatic news at the sports banquet combine to create another great story by Coach Clair Bee.

Be sure to read *Pitchers' Duel,* the seventh book in the Chip Hilton Sports series.

Afterword

I WAS FORTUNATE to have older brothers, because as I was becoming an avid reader in the early 1960s our family's bookcase already contained a selection of well-worn Chip Hilton books. Bob and Sam Walker had un-wittingly provided me a great learning treasure. Once I read my first Hilton book, I was hooked. I read them all, faster than you can say "Hardy Boys." And because I had access to Chip, Speed Morris, Coach Rockwell, and all the other characters and situations that Clair Bee created for his protagonist, the manner that Chip dealt with adversity and people had a significant influence on my understanding of sports, competition, and life.

Chip always had challenges—not just on the field or the court, but in dealing with the hardships of everyday life. He came from a single parent household. He and his mother, Mary Hilton, had lost Big Chip years before young Chip became a legend at Valley Falls High. Money was tight and young Chip never shirked his responsibility to help support the family. But there were temptations. As Chip's athletic prowess grew, someone was always trying to slip him a little extra cash in the time- honored tradition of amateur athletics. But Chip always had a clear sense of right and wrong. Sure he would have liked to help his family and lighten his mother's load. But help meant working at the Sugar Bowl in his spare time or taking a rigorous summer job, never accepting an illicit payment for his athletic skills. Work itself was to be respected, whether it was honing his sport skills through repetition or working the summer before his senior year in high school at the Mansfield Steel Mill. There was never a substitute for hard work, never a sense of entitlement, no matter how successful Chip became.

Chip also faced plenty of adversity at Valley Falls High and State University as he battled to help his teams win. His adversaries did not always exhibit the integrity and fair play that hallmarked Chip's life. But Chip never stopped to play their devious games. And Chip would never back down from a challenge no matter how unfair. It just made the challenge a little tougher and the victory a little sweeter.

There were plenty of victories over the years. Chip had been blessed with athletic greatness to go along with the mental toughness and the strong character that he had developed. Yet he remained humble. He was respectful to coaches, teammates, and other people who could not necessarily help him advance his career. He was a star athlete who won great acclaim but who was still loved and respected, not envied, by those who knew him best. He was always willing to share credit and fully understood that the team needed help from all its contributors to succeed. The obvious conclusion that Chip had reached was that teammates should be rewarded for their efforts, even if they weren't grabbing the headlines, as he did. Chip in return, got unmitigated support from those friends when the going got tough.

Were Chip's experiences too idealistic? Perhaps a little. After all, girls were never a big part of his life and Chip's teams won a disproportionately high percentage of their games, in every sport. I prefer to focus on the character, the integrity, the hard work, the teamwork, the humility, and the respect for others that are described in Clair Bee's books. And indeed these attributes are loftily ideal, always challenging. But the more that we are reminded of the potential that these characteristics hold for success, not just in sports but in life, the better. I plan on making the Chip Hilton series readily available for my children's reading, just as my brothers did for me more than thirty years ago.

WALLY WALKER
President and General Manager, Seattle Supersonics

more great releases from the

by Coach Clair Bee

The sports-loving boy, born out of the imagination of Clair Bee, is back! Clair Bee first began writing the Chip Hilton Series in 1948. During the next twenty years, over two million copies of the series were sold. Written in the tradition of the *Hardy Boys* mysteries, each book in this 23-volume series is a positive–themed tale of human relationships, good sportsmanship, and positive influences — things especially crucial to young boys in the '90s. Through these larger-than-life fictional characters, countless young people have been exposed to stories that helped shape their lives.

WELCOME BACK, CHIP HILTON!

TOUCHDOWN PASS
#1
0-8054-1686-2

CHAMPIONSHIP BALL
#2
0-8054-1815-6

available at fine bookstores everywhere

more great releases from the

Chip Hilton Sports Series

by Coach Clair Bee

The sports-loving boy, born out of the imagination of Clair Bee, is back! Clair Bee first began writing the Chip Hilton Series in 1948. During the next twenty years, over two million copies of the series were sold. Written in the tradition of the *Hardy Boys* mysteries, each book in this 23-volume series is a positive-themed tale of human relationships, good sportsmanship, and positive influences — things especially crucial to young boys in the '90s. Through these larger-than-life fictional characters, countless young people have been exposed to stories that helped shape their lives.

WELCOME BACK, CHIP HILTON!